"Knock it off," Weiss said as he rushed Sydney. This time he managed to throw her off Parker. The man was bloodied and bruised, but still standing. Weiss didn't have the time to notice anything else. Sydney was on him in a flash.

Weiss blocked most of her blows, but he couldn't have landed a punch in return if he had tried. The inability to fight wasn't physical; it was mental. He couldn't bring himself to hurt her. It was quickly becoming clear to him that Sydney was under the influence of Sway. It was the only logical possibility.

"I said stop!" Weiss yelled as he managed to get both hands on her and pushed her back into the kitchen, slamming her into the refrigerator.

Sydney hesitated for a moment, but then pushed back, sending Weiss tumbling to the ground. As he lay there looking up at Sydney, she jumped over him, going for Parker once again. The DEA agent was reaching for his gun.

"No!" Weiss yelled.

ALIAS™

THE

SERIES

MIND GAMES

BY PAUL RUDITIS

An original novel based on the hit TV series created by J. J. Abrams

SSE

SIMON SPOTLIGHT ENTERTAINMENT

New York London Toronto Sydney

SSE

SIMON SPOTLIGHT ENTERTAINMENT
An imprint of Simon & Schuster
1230 Avenue of the Americas, New York, New York 10020

Manufactured in the United States of America
First Edition 10 9 8 7 6 5 4 3 2 1
Library of Congress Control Number 2006925830
ISBN-13: 978-1-4169-2445-6
ISBN-10: 1-4169-2445-0

For Rita, Nancy, Lou, Tim, and Helen

ALIAS™

CHAPTER 1

NEW YORK

The driving beat of techno pounded in Sydney's ears. A current of pulsing bumps and thuds accompanied by synthetic music and electronic voices singing the same line over and over again drummed into her brain. She wondered when this kind of music had become the soundtrack of her life. The repetitive dance beat followed her everywhere she went. It stuck in her head long after she left whatever club she had last been in. It haunted her dreams. She even found herself walking in time with the silent beat every now and again. It had to stop.

"I wonder if I can get workman's comp," Sydney mumbled aloud.

Amazingly, the waitress picking up drinks beside her could actually hear what Sydney said to herself over the echoing beat. "Problem?" the dark-haired, scantily dressed woman asked.

"Repetitive music syndrome," Sydney replied. "I was wondering if I could be compensated for the damage this music is doing to my health."

"Good question," the waitress said. "But I suspect the effects are cumulative, so you won't actually show any measurable signs until you're eighty."

"Oh, good. Something to look forward to," Sydney replied. "By then this club will have closed and forty or fifty others would have opened and closed in its place."

The waitress flashed Sydney an understanding smile, then circled the club, dropping off drinks, taking new orders, and checking IDs. Thankfully the woman didn't get too inquisitive with who she must have assumed was "the new girl," since Sydney didn't really work at the club.

"Sounds like you've made a friend," Dixon's voice said to her over the comm.

"All in the course of blending in," Sydney replied,

keeping a watchful eye on her partner, who was sitting at a small table on the raised platform across the room. In her black sequined top, red leather pants, and bright red wig with blue highlights, she did pretty well blending in with the patrons of the club. Of course the extreme makeup and strategically placed piercings helped her already youthful face look even younger. Poor Dixon didn't have a chance in the place, which is why he didn't even bother to try.

"You're far too young to be complaining about this music," Dixon said. "Now imagine if you were my age."

"I always thought hearing was the first thing to go in a man of your advanced years," Sydney joked. "This music shouldn't be bothering you at all."

"You'll pay for that," Dixon replied. She could hear the laughter in his voice.

Sydney took another visual pass of the room. She thought—not for the first time—that it was an odd place to have a meet. Cube was one of the trendiest new clubs in the Village, all black lacquer and chrome, with a DJ spinning the requisite house music. Sydney had spent more than enough time in clubs around the globe to have a whole catalog of electronica stored in her brain. These kinds of "hot" nightspots were de rigueur for illegal operations around the world. The idea of setting the meet in a nightclub was not the odd part, and it wasn't just the music that was making her feel her age.

Cube was an underage club—a place for the eighteen and up set to go and party down like the rock stars they wished they were. The patrons were advertised as a mix of the hottest teens and coolest young adults. Not surprisingly, the ads were done in such a way that would make any adults who entered the club feel like they were staging a pathetic attempt at remaining "cool." Consequently, there didn't look to be anyone over the age of twenty in the place aside from Dixon. Sydney, at least, was able to blend in with the staff, but she had already watched Dixon receive more than one curious—and snotty—glance from the kids around him.

"Norwood just entered," Dixon said over the comm.

"I've got him," Sydney said as she turned her attention to the entrance, where she found a man who looked exactly like his surveillance photos. The same black slicked-back hair. The same poor choice in flashy attire. Exactly the type of person the club owners wanted to deter. "He's spotted you."

"I'm shocked," Dixon deadpanned. "How did he ever pick me out of this crowd?"

It wasn't hard to track the forty-year-old man as he made his way through the teens. It helped that most of them were giving him a wide berth, as if his age might rub off on them. It only made what was happening behind him all the more noticeable.

Far from ignoring him, the kids coming into the club behind Malcolm Norwood were treating him like he was the Pied Piper. Their eyes followed him across the room. And it wasn't because he was so ancient at forty. Something had happened outside. That much Sydney could tell from the way the kids were eagerly talking and pointing when they met up with their friends inside. Sydney was tempted to check it out, but figured she should stay with Dixon until she was sure the meet was secure.

Sydney continued to watch as Norwood made his approach. Even with the loud music, she could clearly hear every word when Norwood reached the table. Once again, she was impressed by the abilities of op-tech genius, Marshall J. Flinkman.

"Mr. Marsch?" Norwood said as he stood above Dixon.

"Now how did you find me here so quickly?" Dixon joked as he indicated that Norwood should take a seat. "I must say this isn't the best place to conduct our business. We do stand out somewhat."

"I know," Norwood replied. "But I assure you there's a method to my madness."

"I should hope," Dixon said.

Sydney took that as her cue to put her alias to work for her. She raised her empty tray and made her way to Dixon's table to take an order. It wasn't an easy walk through the popular club, which was packed wall-to-wall with posturing kids.

"Hey, waitress!" A pretty boy—dressed in shredded clothing that his parents obviously shelled out a fortune for, so he could look homeless—grabbed Sydney's arm. "My friends and I want—"

"Sorry. Not my section," she breezily replied as she pushed past him and continued through the crowd. She didn't get far before she felt another set of fingers wrap around her arm. Instinctively she prepared to attack, but held herself back when she realized it was the same pretty boy.

"Now, now," he said. "That's no way to keep the customers happy. Besides, I tip *very* well." He did something with his eyes Sydney assumed was supposed to look suggestive, but didn't. "Now, we'd like a round of martinis."

Sydney tried not to burst out laughing as she considered all the ways she could kill this obnoxious child. Thankfully, she didn't have to deal with kids like him for a living. She remained calm as she heard over the comm that her waitress friend from earlier had already beaten her to the punch and was taking Dixon and Norwood's order.

Since he had already cost her the opportunity to get a closer inspection of Norwood, Sydney turned back to the pretty boy, planning to give him the kind of service he so rightfully deserved. "ID please."

"Sure," her would-be customer said as he held up a hundred-dollar bill.

Sydney looked at the picture of Benjamin Franklin, then at the pretty boy. "Wow. You don't look half as good as your photo." At this, his friends busted up like it was the funniest thing they had ever heard. Sydney figured not many people usually called the kid out on his crap.

"The drinks," he insisted.

"Sure," Sydney said, leaving the hundred behind as she continued her walk through the club. She had no intention of delivering drinks, but she didn't need the distraction any longer. It was time to get back to work, making sure that no one was too interested in the meeting. Not that any of the teens seemed to belong to any international crime syndicates. *Then again, they are being recruited younger and younger these days.*

As she focused on the task at hand, Sydney was glad to hear that while she had been dealing with the pretty boy, Dixon had made his offer. Norwood claimed to have information that the United States government desperately wanted returned.

"I was thinking something more along the lines of twice that amount," Norwood replied, "as an *opening* bid."

"That is more money than I had anticipated for some stolen computer files," Dixon said after hearing Norwood's counteroffer. "I think you're overestimating the value."

"Oh, I'm not offering the files," Norwood said. "I'm offering the *results* of the research."

"Results?" Dixon asked. Sydney knew that this was as much a surprise to him as it was to her. The documents had only been stolen from the government lab a month earlier.

All signs had pointed to Malcolm Norwood as the thief of the documents. A series of former contacts led Dixon, working under an alias, to Malcolm Norwood's undisclosed e-mail account. The thief proudly confirmed what they had suspected. He had been the one to break into the secret FBI research lab and steal the files. He claimed to have given those files over to his buyer, but was willing to entertain any offers Dixon might want to make in the interest of obtaining that information himself.

At no time had anyone in the black ops unit, known as APO—Authorized Personnel Only—guessed that the files had been put to use. If what Sydney's boss, Arvin Sloane, had been told was correct, the files weren't even complete. There was no way the buyer could have used them—unless this mystery person Norwood was working for already had something in development and only needed the FBI research files to put on the finishing touches.

"Results," Norwood confirmed with a grin that Sydney could see from across the room. The man obviously knew he had Dixon's attention. "The buyer I procured those files for has been very busy. He took the government's failures and actually made something of them."

"And what, exactly, is that?" Dixon asked.

"A drug unlike anything you've ever seen," Norwood said. "How many of these kids do you think are on some party cocktail right this very minute?"

"I'm not a drug dealer," Dixon said.

"You could be," Norwood replied, looking smug. "It's called Sway. I think it was supposed to start out as a derivative of E or something, but then it became oh-so-much more."

"And this person you represent—"

"Oh no," Norwood said. "Sorry for the confusion, but I'm a free agent on this."

"The person who created Sway is out of the picture?" Dixon asked.

"It's more like a case of Sway has been taken out of *his* picture," Norwood said. "And I know where I can get even more."

"So you're offering me stolen goods?"

"Stolen files? Stolen drugs? Why quibble?" Norwood said. "The point is . . . this is an amazing opportunity."

Sydney was intrigued by this development, but she and Dixon weren't interested in a drug deal. They needed to retrieve the missing files. Sydney couldn't imagine what kind of drugs the secret research lab had been developing, but that wasn't part of the original job. They were just supposed to get the files, not ask what was in them.

At the same time, now that they knew a drug had resulted from those stolen files, they couldn't just leave it out on the streets. Now they had to get the files and the drugs. But there was no reason Norwood needed to know how anxious Dixon was to acquire both.

Dixon started to get up from his chair. "If you don't have the complete files—"

"Wait!" Norwood said eagerly. "I've arranged a little show for you, to give you an idea of what Sway can do."

"I've witnessed people on drugs before," Dixon said. His voice sounded like he was uninterested, but he sat back in his chair all the same.

"Not like this," Norwood said as he motioned to a blond girl in a short silver dress. She looked barely old enough to pass for eighteen. Sydney recognized her as one of the kids that had come in behind Norwood when he entered the club.

The girl immediately came over to him. "We need to liven this place up," he said to her. "What this joint needs is some real dancing. What say you get up on that bar and show them how it's done?"

"Sure," the girl said.

Sydney watched as the girl approached her at the bar. The girl's eyes seemed focused and alert. There wasn't a hint that she was on anything at all. But at the same time, she did exactly as Norwood told her. She gently pushed a boy out of the way, climbed on a barstool and then up onto the bar, gyrating to the music without a care. The bartender seemed equally as annoyed as he was amused, but he let her dance. The audience around her loved it.

Still, it wasn't proof that the girl was on any kind of drug as far as Sydney was concerned. Norwood could have just made an arrangement with the girl to do what he told her. He could have paid her off outside the club, which might have been what she was telling her friends about him when she had come in. It didn't mean she was on anything. Sydney listened as Dixon echoed that concern over the mike.

"Oh, so you want a real show?" Norwood asked. Sydney did not like the eagerly playful tone in his voice as he called a boy over to the table. She couldn't hear the words that were exchanged between the pair, but she could tell by the satisfied look on Norwood's face that it wasn't good. She especially didn't like it when the boy headed up the stairs to the balcony level above. Norwood had whispered his instructions to the boy, so it wasn't clear what he was about to do, but Sydney had her suspicions.

Sydney followed the boy up to the balcony level of the club. The place was less densely packed up there, probably due to the rising heat from the dance floor below making it a less accommodating place. The few people in the darkened balcony were mostly paired up and interested only in each other. They paid no attention to the guy walking through them. Sydney watched the boy climb up on the balcony rail looking like he was about to swan dive onto the people down below.

Sydney rushed across the balcony and grabbed onto the kid's belt. "Whoa, there," she said, pulling him down. "You don't want to do that."

"Okay," the kid said as he simply turned away and went back downstairs as if nothing had happened.

"How was that?" Norwood's voice asked over the comm.

"Well, you've gotten my attention," Dixon said. "But I'm still not sold."

"You want me to have some kid kill another one?" Norwood asked. "Because I could do it. I could get half the kids here to do things they normally wouldn't consider any other time. That's the power of Sway."

"So, you've got a drug that lowers people's inhibitions," Dixon said, downplaying the events.

"I've got a drug that makes people do things against their will," Norwood clarified. "Anything they are told. Imagine the possibilities."

Norwood didn't need to say that last part. Sydney was already imagining. The fact that Norwood was playing parlor games with kids only showed that he didn't really imagine the *true* possibilities. If Sway was everything he was promising, it was the ultimate mind-control drug. In the wrong hands it could be used for much darker purposes than dancing on bars.

Sydney took a position at the balcony rail and continued to watch from above as the waitress returned with Dixon and Norwood's drinks. There really wasn't concrete proof that the drug was what Norwood promised, but she knew Dixon wouldn't risk letting the guy use it on any more of the kids.

"How does it work?" Dixon asked.

Norwood leaned back in his chair, satisfied that he had Dixon on the hook. "Beats me. I just sell the stuff."

"So you're offering me something you don't know anything about," Dixon said.

"I know enough," Norwood said. "I know what Sway can do. I know that you give it to someone and they are completely at your mercy. They'll do whatever you want. And when you're done, they'll just sleep it off and no one will be any the wiser. But the most important thing I know is how to get more."

"I may be interested in Sway," Dixon said. "But I still want the original files and what other secrets they may reveal. Why don't we agree to this: I will buy your boxful for a very good price, so long as it comes with the location of your original buyer so I can make him an offer for the files as well."

"And let him know that I stole his stuff?" Norwood asked skeptically.

"I can leave that out," Dixon said.

Norwood only considered the offer for a

moment. "How about this: You buy my shipment. I'll steal back the files and then you can buy those, too."

"Take the deal, Dixon," Sydney said. "Now that we've got a location on Norwood we can track him back to the buyer."

Dixon nodded to both Norwood and Sydney. Even from above she could see the look of joyful relief wash over Norwood as he took a swig of his drink, finishing it off in one gulp.

"Well, this certainly has been a pleasure," Norwood said as he reached into his jacket pocket and pulled out his phone. "Sorry," he apologized to Dixon. At first Sydney thought he was calling someone to make arrangements, but Norwood checked the caller ID screen before he opened the phone. Someone was calling him. It must have been set on vibrate because it would have been impossible to hear a ring over the music. "Hello!" he called into the mouthpiece, then sat silently for a few seconds before saying "I understand" and hanging up.

Sydney continued to watch as he put the phone back in his jacket and pulled out a gun. She considered jumping down from the balcony to protect

Dixon, but the gun was not aimed in his direction.

Dixon was immediately out of his seat trying to stop the man. "Norwood, no!"

But it was too late. Norwood put the gun to his temple and pulled the trigger.

CHAPTER 2

Sydney couldn't hear the pop of the gun over the music, but she did see the spray of blood hit a trio of girls at the next table. At first they looked annoyed, probably thinking someone had spilled a drink on them. Then realization hit as they looked down at their clothes and one another. And then the screaming started. Their high-pitched screeching caught the attention of other kids nearby, who soon joined in the chorus. Sydney watched as, one by one, every kid in the area turned in Norwood's direction as his body fell to the floor.

The screaming multiplied exponentially as the club patrons ran for the door. Panic spread throughout Cube as more and more of the teens started screaming and pushing their way out. Most of them couldn't have seen what had happened, but Sydney knew fear was contagious. Their bodies instinctively reacted to the inherent danger. They were reacting to the fear of fear itself.

Sydney looked over the rail and saw that Dixon was searching Norwood's body, presumably for the samples of Sway. But she had other things on her mind. The caller had to be inside the building—how else could the person have known to make the call as soon as Norwood finished his drink, which had clearly been laced with the drug?

Sydney knew she'd never find anyone in the swarming mass of teens trying to escape the club. With all the panicking bodies running in the same direction, it just became a sea of heads from Sydney's vantage point. But then she realized she already knew the identity of the person she had to find. She knew the color of the hair on the top of the head she was looking for.

The call had been made a moment after Norwood

took his drink. And only one person would have known which drink was his.

Sydney turned her attention to the far side of the bar where most of the staff had gathered. They all had the same clueless look on their faces, clearly wondering what to do about the panicking kids. On the opposite side of the room, the bouncers and club owner were trying desperately to maintain control of the entrance to avoid injury and lawsuits. But one employee wasn't with either of the groups. The waitress Sydney had spoken with earlier was sneaking out the back door behind the bar. She wasn't panicking like the rest of the club goers. She was simply strolling along as if nothing out of the ordinary was happening around her.

"Outrigger, I've got the caller," Sydney said into her mike as she raced to the stairs. She was glad that the balcony had been practically empty. No one got in her way until she reached ground level. And even then all the kids were heading for the main entrance. Apparently none of them had caught on to the fact that there was a back door. *All the better for me,* Sydney thought as she pushed her way through the straggling kids, hopped over the bar, and went out through the back.

Sydney pulled her gun from her thigh holster as she exited to the alley. To the right was a dead end. To the left was the street where kids were already screaming out into the night, running between cars and forcing drivers to slam on the brakes. Blaring horns added to the cacophony as patrons mixed with traffic. Sydney raced out to the street, but she knew she was already too late. With kids running in every direction, it was impossible to tell where the waitress could have gone. Sydney continued to scan the streets looking for the dark-haired woman. But it was already pointless.

Dixon came running up the alley behind her. "Was it the waitress?"

"I'm pretty sure," Sydney said. "But I lost her."

"That's okay," Dixon said. "Look what I got." He held up a key card for the Hotel Twenty-Nine. It was the newest and trendiest of the few hotels in SoHo. It figured that a man like Norwood would be staying there.

Sydney grabbed the key card from him. "You go secure the body," she instructed as she slipped her gun back into the holster. "I'll take care of this."

"Be careful," Dixon warned as she took off.

Hotel Twenty-Nine was only a few blocks away.

Sydney ran the entire way. The streets were packed, but it didn't slow her down too much as she rushed between cars in the stop-and-go traffic to avoid the slow-moving people on the sidewalks. She slowed to a brisk walk as she turned the corner onto the street the hotel was on. Sydney relaxed her breathing so that she didn't look out of place among the trendy guests and strolled up to the front of the hotel. The doorman held one of the glass doors open for her, nodding hello with barely a glance at her painted-on clothing and shiny silver body jewelry. Even though she was in an outfit that wasn't exactly tame, Sydney knew, considering the guests this place normally attracted, she wasn't going to stand out in the least.

Like in most hotels in the city, the lobby was relatively small—all sleek lines and modern furniture. Sydney ignored the decor and walked straight to the front desk. There, a young couple in even tighter clothing than Sydney's was fighting with the desk clerk. Apparently, the rail-thin man was outraged over the fact that their room was on an odd-numbered floor. The woman just seemed angry in general.

Sydney tuned out the ridiculous fight while she

tried to figure out a way to push past them without adding to the delay. Once she determined that anything she did would only make it worse, she just waited while the desk clerk switched their room.

After the annoying couple finally left, Sydney approached the desk wearing a friendly look on her face. "That was *crazy*," she said with a bubbly lilt in her voice. "I don't know how you put up with jerks like that."

"At Hotel Twenty-Nine we strive to make everyone's stay enjoyable," the clerk said with an intentionally plastic smile on his face. "Now, how may I help *you*?"

Sydney forced a flirtatious laugh to play along. Like many of the employees in hotels like this, the clerk looked like he was a struggling model by day. Most likely, he was hired to look hot and be flirtatious. He'd probably be glad to see his work was paying off when someone flirted back. "Well, I'm hoping you *can* help me," Sydney said.

"What seems to be the problem?" he asked. "Have you been placed on an even-numbered floor against your will?"

"*No!*" She laughed again as she waved the keycard in front him. "My boyfriend's visiting me this week. *From L.A.* And my roommate doesn't like him staying with us when he's here, see? So he comes to your nice hotel instead. Now, we're partying in the neighborhood tonight and I told him I need to freshen up a bit. And since this hotel's way closer than my tiny apartment he gave me his room key so I could clean up a little."

"Okay," the clerk said, clearly wondering where this was going.

"So he gives me his key," Sydney continued, "but he never tells me his room number. But that's Mal for ya. Never thinking more than a half step ahead of hisself. So, I was wondering, is it possible for you to tell me what room he's in?"

"Certainly," the desk clerk said as he took the keycard and slid it through the card reader. He looked up the information on the screen. "What is the guest's name?"

"Mal," Sydney replied. "Sorry. I mean . . . Mal*colm*. Malcolm Norwood."

The desk clerk confirmed the information on the screen and nodded that she had gotten it right. Sydney was relieved to know that Norwood hadn't registered under an alias.

"He's in room twelve thirty," the desk clerk said as he handed back the keycard.

"Thanks a *bunch*," she said as she blew him a kiss. Sydney sauntered to the elevator, knowing that he was watching her the entire time. When the elevator arrived, she turned back and gave the guy an exaggerated wink. Then she stepped inside, pressed twelve, and rode up to the floor. It only took her a minute to get to Norwood's room.

Sydney slipped the key into the lock and waited for the light to turn green, but nothing happened. She removed the key and tried it again. And again, nothing happened. Sydney wondered if the desk clerk had gotten the room right. Figuring the third time could be the charm, Sydney wiped the key card off and tried again. This time, the door unlocked. With a shrug, she entered the hotel room.

Much like the lobby, the room was a typical New York hotel room, meaning small. But that wasn't the first thing to draw Sydney's attention. Either Malcolm Norwood was a first-class slob, or somebody had beaten her to the room. All the drawers were hanging open. The bedding was on the floor and the mattress was askew. Someone had already given the room a very quick once-over.

When Sydney noticed that the bathroom door was ajar, she pulled out her gun and cautiously moved toward it. Unfortunately, she would never make it to her target. The waitress from the club burst out of the closet, swinging an iron at Sydney's head.

Sydney barely had time to register the fact that it was the woman she had been looking for as she ducked and felt the breeze as the iron passed inches from her skull. She popped up with a fist to the woman's gut. It was like hitting concrete. The woman countered by kicking Sydney's legs out from under her. Sydney fell back into the wall as the woman followed up with a second kick. This time she was aiming for Sydney's stomach. When Sydney doubled over in pain, the woman brought the iron down on the back of Sydney's head, knocking her unconscious and ending the fight as quickly as it had begun.

CHAPTER 3

LOS ANGELES

"Arvin Sloane hates me."

"He doesn't hate you," Michael Vaughn said. "He just doesn't know you yet."

Eric Weiss found little solace in his friend's words as they walked through the bright white and glass halls of the APO bunker underneath the City of Angels. "Oh please. The man can't stand me. The only reason I'm on this team is because I stumbled across you guys accidentally when I got captured on a mission. Do you even know what it feels like to be picked last for a team? Oh, what am

I saying? You're the golden boy, Vaughn. You were never picked last in your life. Hell, I wasn't picked at all. I got the booby prize for being in the wrong place at the right time."

"And to what do we owe this descent into self-pity?" Vaughn asked. "Did something happen between you and Sloane or is this just a general freak-out?"

"Why would you think something happened? Did you hear about something happening?" Weiss asked, knowing he sounded totally guilty. Luckily they had just reached the APO medical center and would have to table the discussion for the moment.

"You called us, Dr. Jain?" Weiss asked as they entered the medical center. He could see the body of Malcolm Norwood laid out on the slab in the adjoining room. Dixon had done some fast talking at the scene of the crime—and flashed a false badge—to get Norwood's body released to him and sent to APO. All of this was done within the span of twenty-four hours, which was pretty impressive, in view of how red tape usually slowed anything and everything in their line of work. Considering that APO was a black ops division of the CIA, *officially* reporting to no one, it was amazing how much typical bureaucracy still managed to have an impact on their daily lives.

Dixon had obviously known which strings to pull, because the NYPD had shipped out the body in record time. The former thief's chest was open in a *Y*-shaped cut on the examining table, where his innards were exposed to the world. For not the first time Weiss wished that they worked in a regular office building with solid walls and doors. He was also glad that he had skipped lunch that afternoon.

The good doctor was busy at a microscope, but put his work on hold for the moment to address the agents. "Yes, I've finished the preliminary autopsy."

"Let me guess," Weiss said. "He died of a bullet wound to the head."

Dr. Jain just looked at him. Weiss had, once again, forgotten that the man didn't have much of a sense of humor.

"You'll have to excuse Weiss," Vaughn said. "He's experiencing some work-related stress at the moment."

"It's not just work related. 'Work related' is now 'personal life related,' if you know what I mean," Weiss said.

"Actually, I have no idea what you're talking

about," Dr. Jain said before leading them into the room with the body. "I did a full workup but couldn't find anything in Mr. Norwood's system. There was no trace of any drugs in his stomach or his blood. Anywhere."

"He had to be on something," Weiss said as he and Vaughn followed. "Nobody just answers the phone and shoots himself. That'd be one hell of a wrong number."

"I'm not saying he hadn't been affected by this mystery drug," Dr. Jain said. "Sway, is it? However this drug is supposed to affect this man, it was no longer in his system by the time his body got here. More than eighteen hours had passed between the time of death and his arrival on my table. Sometimes drugs like these are designed to break down without a trace."

"That's not good," Weiss said, knowing that he was stating the obvious.

"Exactly," Dr. Jain agreed. "If this Sway is some kind of mind-control drug, what better way to frame someone for a crime? By the time you'd take a blood sample, the drug will have left the victim's system. No way to prove he had been acting against his will."

"Well, that's a cheery thought," Vaughn said.

"At least the effects are short-lived," Weiss said. "According to Dixon, Norwood said something about sleeping it off?"

"I can't tell you the cure if I don't know the drug," Dr. Jain said apologetically. "I'll have a full report in time for the briefing, but I don't expect much more at this point."

"Thanks," Vaughn said.

"Yeah, thanks, doc," Weiss added as they left the medical center. He was glad to be out of the room with the body. Weiss had seen a lot of death during his career. It was something he still hadn't gotten used to. But that was nothing compared to seeing the aftereffects of death spread out before him on an examining-room table.

"Well, that got us nowhere," he added once the door shut behind them. "Why'd we have to come down here in the first place? Couldn't he have just told us that over the phone?"

"A little tense there, buddy?"

"Noticed, huh?"

"You can't let Sloane get to you," Vaughn said. "It's probably all in your imagination. You do have a fairly active fantasy life."

"Oh no, I'm pretty sure he hates me," Weiss insisted.

"Did something happen?" Vaughn asked.

Weiss looked around to make sure no one was in earshot. He wouldn't have put it past Sloane to have the whole place bugged. Weiss knew that back when Sloane was the head of the terrorist organization SD-6, he'd loaded the whole place with surveillance equipment. It wouldn't be difficult for him to do the same thing at APO. Even though the organization was ultrablack ops, that didn't mean that Arvin Sloane wasn't keeping tabs on things.

Aside from that concern, they did work with a group of people who made surveillance a life mission. Having this conversation in the middle of a hall was not the best idea. Anyone could be listening. Weiss pulled his friend into the nearest empty office.

"Okay, here's the deal," Weiss said after he shut the glass door. Once again, he wished for opaque walls. "As you know, Nadia and I seem to have a little sparkage going on between us."

"It's nice to know that you've moved on to more mature adult relationships," Vaughn said. "With your 'sparkage' and all. Are you thinking about giving her your class ring and asking her to go steady?"

"Anyway," Weiss continued, "I was impressing her with one of my powers of prestidigitation—"

"You were doing some card tricks," Vaughn interrupted, enjoying this way more than he had any right to.

"Not mere card tricks," Weiss said, insulted. "I was breaking out the big guns, when Mr. Sloane happened by."

"Not exactly a sentence I ever wanted to hear."

"Of course, Nadia was so impressed that she insisted I show him the trick."

"Please tell me it wasn't the one where you smash a watch in a pouch."

"No," Weiss said, offended by the suggestion. "It was the one where I cut a tie in half and put it back together."

Vaughn didn't even bother to hold back his laughter as he came to his own conclusion. "Aw, man. You *are* screwed."

"Totally screwed," Weiss said woefully. He still remembered the look on Sloane's face while he stood holding two separate parts of one tie. This was not a man one liked to make angry. Arvin Sloane had been responsible for the deaths of countless people over the years. Surely one of those people had done something innocent, like ruined his favorite tie, and was punished for it. What was one more body in Sloane's wake?

"And why are you laughing at me?" Weiss asked, rightfully feeling indignant. He'd been through similar conversations with Vaughn before, during which his friend had been on the other side of the equation. "Seems like you don't have a much better relationship with *your* girlfriend's father."

"She's not my girlfriend," Vaughn said. "We're taking it slow."

"Yeah, whatever," Weiss said. He still didn't understand why Vaughn and Sydney were playing that game. They were still together. It was like they thought if they didn't put a name on their relationship then it wouldn't be doomed in the many ways it had been in the past. Never in his life had Weiss seen two people so destined to be together suffer as much as his closest friends. "Seriously though," Weiss continued, "how did you get in good with Jack?"

"What makes you think I have?" Vaughn asked.

"I'm serious, man."

"So am I," Vaughn said with a sigh. "Look. The one thing Jack has always respected is when I stand up for myself. He doesn't like weakness. Sloane is the same way. The best thing you can do is show Sloane that you care about Nadia and you won't give up on her just because he intimidates you."

"He doesn't *intimidate* me," Weiss said defensively. Vaughn just looked at him in disbelief. "Okay. He intimidates the hell out of me."

"And stick to card tricks," Vaughn added.

"Why couldn't we fall for girls with dads who are puny little accountant types?" Weiss asked.

"Because we wouldn't be interested in the kinds of girls who are the daughters of puny little accountant types. We like the challenge of women with deeply rooted father issues."

Weiss nodded his head solemnly in agreement. "Sad, but true, my friend. Sad, but true."

"I think my father hates Eric," Nadia Santos said.

"He doesn't hate Eric," Sydney replied. "He just doesn't know Eric yet." Granted, Sydney didn't really know how Arvin Sloane felt about anyone, so she was the last person who should be reassuring her half sister of anything. But it was more important at the moment that Nadia felt she had someone on her side. She was having a hard enough time adjusting to all of the horrible truths she'd found out about her family history. The last thing she needed was to think that her burgeoning relationship with Eric Weiss was doomed from the start because of her father of all people.

"No, it's more than that," Nadia insisted. "He has this look on his face whenever Eric comes into a room. I can't really describe it."

"Are you talking about the look where his eyes burn into your very soul or the one where it's like he ate something that disagreed with him?" Marshall Flinkman asked, making faces that matched each description. "You know, like a small child." His face switched back and forth between the two looks, adding a considerable amount of unintentional levity to the conversation.

"More like a combination of the two," Nadia replied as Marshall's face froze mid-switch. He had obviously been practicing making funny faces with his young son.

"Mr. Sloane's like that with everyone," Marshall said offhandedly. "It took me three years to get over the feeling that he wouldn't hesitate to kill me if I made a mistake. Of course, then he went all überevil and probably *would* have killed me for no reason. But now that he's good again—or at least we think he's good again—he's back to his normal old tense self."

"Thanks, Marshall," Nadia said in a tone that didn't sound thankful in the least. Sydney wished Marshall had a better censor when he spoke. Nadia really didn't need to be reminded about the "überevil" nature of her father's past. Of course, Sydney couldn't manage to wipe it from her own mind, no matter how much she tried.

"Why don't we talk about this later?" Sydney suggested. She wasn't sure Nadia was up for Marshall's particular brand of cheering up—zany faces aside. "I want to get this mystery woman identified."

"Just one more second," Marshall said as he tapped various keys on his computer keyboard with blurring speed. "Still working out the glitches on this new sketch program I put together. It's light-years ahead of anything on the market . . . when it's working, that is."

"Are you sure we shouldn't just go with a good old-fashioned paper sketch?" Sydney asked. "Or use the old program? We're supposed to brief in half an hour."

"It'll just be another minute," Marshall said.

Sydney didn't like how his "one more second" had just jumped to a minute, but she didn't say anything. Marshall got so enthusiastic over his tech toys that she hated to stop him. The look of disappointment on his face when he thought he had failed her was unbearable.

"How's your head, by the way?" Nadia asked. "Has the swelling gone down?"

"Not that I've noticed," Sydney said. She was wearing her hair up in a bun to cover the extreme lump on the back of her head. That iron had done quite a number on her. Sydney had been out for twenty minutes before she heard Dixon's voice in her ear calling out to her over the comm. By the time she awoke, the dark-haired nonwaitress was gone, and the room had been tossed even worse than when Sydney had originally entered. There was no trace of any drug on the premises—or any secret FBI files, for that matter. "I can't wait to get my hands on that woman in a real fight," Sydney added.

"Maybe you could arm yourself with a Cuisinart," Marshall suggested. "You know . . . as opposed to an iron."

Sydney and Nadia just looked at him, not responding to the joke.

"Almost got it," Marshall said as he went back to typing. "You know, considering how you were also posing as a waitress, that club really needs to track its employees better. Or maybe they just don't mind the extra help."

"Did we get a trace off Norwood's phone?" Nadia asked, ignoring Marshall's latest subject switch.

"The number was blocked," Sydney replied.

"Not just blocked," Marshall added. "Bounced from here to New Delhi with stops at all points north, south, east, *and* west." Marshall punctuated his statement by pressing the return key. This brought up the partial computer sketch they had been working on before the program had shut down.

The three-dimensional image of the woman's face was remarkably lifelike and considerably similar to the one Sydney had met at the club and seen briefly afterward. The light skin, blue eyes, and small mouth looked almost like parts of an actual photo rather than a computer rendering. Of course, after the blow to the head, Sydney did question whether she was remembering it correctly. They would have to run the image by Dixon as well for confirmation. He hadn't seen the waitress as well as Sydney had, but a second pair of eyes wouldn't hurt in this case.

"That really is an amazing program," Sydney said. It was truly impressive, but her comment had more to do with the fact that Marshall fed off praise, particularly from her. And the happier he was, the faster he worked. "Her nose was a little slimmer."

"Check," Marshall said as he tapped a few buttons and the image adjusted itself accordingly onscreen.

"And the chin came down more at a point," Sydney added. "Like this." She made a motion with her hands to explain where the image should be taken in.

"How's this?" Marshall typed in another command, slimming the woman's chin.

"A little too much," Sydney said. "Take it back a bit."

"Like this?"

"Perfect."

"Now the hair," Marshall said, regarding the face that currently was without a coif of any kind. "Although I hear the bald look is in this year for women."

"Not the women in this room," Nadia quickly said.

"Oh, I don't know," Marshall said looking at the sisters. "I think you two would look great in any style . . . or no style at all."

Sydney and Nadia shared a smile.

"Thanks," Sydney said. "But back to the picture. Her hair was black, but I'm pretty certain it was a wig."

"And since people in disguise would naturally shy away from their own hair color, that leads us to varying shades of brown, blond, and red."

"Or any number of unnatural colors people wear nowadays," Nadia added. Sydney thought about the many colors she herself had worn in her numerous aliases over the years. There was something about the woman she had met that didn't seem to fit the experimental hair color mold. Though they had only shared a brief exchange, the woman struck Sydney as a normal-hair-color kind of gal.

"Considering the light skin and blue eyes, I say we start with blond," Sydney said.

"One blonde, coming up," Marshall said. All it took was the tap of one key to give the woman shoulder-length blond hair. "Quite a good picture, if I do say so myself."

"I'd say that was her," Sydney said. "How long will it take you to run the image against what we have in the system?"

"A few minutes," Marshall said as he typed in a few more commands. The image onscreen shrank by half as another window popped up beside it. Within moments, a series of fast-moving pictures shuffled through the new window as Marshall had the computer run the image against every known or suspected criminal in the CIA database.

"That *is* an impressive program," Nadia said, providing Marshall with even more praise.

Marshall's face lit up as he slid his chair to the computer on the other side of his desk. "But the sketch program is only the beginning. Say you want to try out a new alias without having to actually . . . you know . . . try it out. All you have to do is load your image into the computer and voilà." A three-dimensional photo of Marshall came up on the screen. "Now say you want to know what I'll look like as a blond with more Scandinavian features, maybe add a cleft to my chin, and why don't we give me a little scar, too. You know, to give me a roguish past." Marshall continued typing in commands and the computer matched his description. "Quite a dashing fellow, don't you think?" Marshall leaned in beside the screen to give them the before-and-after view.

Sydney was quite impressed by the overall effect. She had seen many similar programs before, but nothing with the kind of clarity Marshall's new system offered. Everything he punched in stayed true to his existing bone structure and facial design and yet made him look totally different at the same time. "Nice," she said.

"Of course, Mitchell's personal favorite is when daddy looks like this." He hit another command and his onscreen face morphed into a heavily made-up clown. Sydney actually found the red and green coloring more disturbing than humorous, but there was no telling what would entertain an infant—or an infant's father, for that matter.

The other computer beeped, pulling their attention back to the original screen. There, the three-dimensional sketch was paired with an actual picture that looked remarkably similar. The only real difference was that the woman's blond hair was a shade lighter and a couple of inches longer in the surveillance image. Otherwise, it was a perfect match, right down to the shape of the chin.

"Felicia DeNoble," Nadia read off the screen. "Ever heard of her?"

"No," Sydney said. "But we've got about twenty-five minutes to learn everything we can."

"You've been on this mission for twenty-four hours straight," Nadia said. "Back and forth across the country and with a concussion to show for it. Why don't you take a few minutes and get some rest before the brief. I can look Felicia up myself."

"I'm okay," Sydney insisted. She had rested on the plane back, after all. Besides, there was only so much resting she was allowed to do with her concussion. "We need to track this drug back to the source. It will be better to have two pairs of eyes going over things."

"Oh, I wasn't planning on going through the files alone," Nadia said with a sly smile. "I'm sure I can find someone to help me."

For the time being, Sydney stopped worrying about her sister's burgeoning relationship with Weiss. Whether or not Arvin Sloane had an opinion on the situation didn't seem to matter. Nadia clearly had things under control as far as her own emotions were concerned.

CHAPTER 4

"While it is true this wasn't one of our more successful missions, we do have a lead on the missing papers," Arvin Sloane said in what had to be the understatement of all understatements. The mission was a complete failure in Sydney's mind. She would have laughed, but her head still hurt a little too much for her to risk it.

Sloane was sitting in his now customary spot at the head of the table in the APO conference room. Sydney couldn't help but think this new table was much more conducive to meetings than the original setup of a lone couch and some chairs that made the place look like the designer was attempting a sixties-style living room. She still suspected that the original decor was the result of Sloane trying too hard to make everyone comfortable in an uncomfortable situation.

The APO unit consisted of her closest friends and family under the direction of her most hated enemy. Every time she was in this room, she was both comforted and disgusted, which was often the way she felt in the world lately. At least she knew that she was working for a greater good most of the time. In this case, trying to keep a horrific drug off the street trumped any feelings of mistrust she had for the man in front of her.

Sydney noticed that Weiss had taken the seat next to Sloane. Sydney wished she could telepathically tell her friend that moves like that were not the way to get on Sloane's good side. Not that he had a good side. Thankfully, Nadia had taken a seat on Sloane's other side, which would hopefully distract him from shooting daggers at Weiss during the brief—if, in fact, Sloane was even aware of Weiss's presence in the first place.

The tension between the two men could be

entirely in Nadia's mind. Sydney understood what it was like to assume things about the way one's father felt. That had caused ceaseless concern in her own relationship, and it was possible that the same could be happening with her sister. Not that Sydney truly believed that for a second. She knew her own father's opinion of Vaughn too well to suspect that what Nadia was going through at the moment was merely a figment of her sister's imagination.

This time, Sydney almost did laugh when she realized that she had taken a seat between Vaughn and her father. The arrangement was probably a coincidence, but she couldn't be sure that her subconscious wasn't working to keep the two men in her life separated. Even though Vaughn and her father seemed to be getting along better lately, she knew full well that the relationship could turn on a dime. Then again, the same could also be said of her own relationship with her father.

Of course all these thoughts left something nagging in the back of her mind that she didn't want to focus on at the moment. Instead, she tried to compartmentalize it beside her head wound, and focus on figuring out what Marshall was doodling on his notepad in his seat beside Dixon. There was no telling what that mad little genius could be coming up with, be it a new way to sift information from illegal wiretaps or a motorized mobile for his child's bedroom. Just once she'd like to take a trip inside his mind to see what actually went on in that crazy mixed-up place. The thought of doing so was at once intriguing and terrifying.

"As you can all imagine, Director Chase was not thrilled to learn that the government's stolen research has come to fruition," Sloane said, pulling Sydney's attention back to the task at hand.

"Maybe if the government was a bit less secretive with its illegal research these things wouldn't happen," Dixon said offhandedly.

"I think we're the last ones to comment on what the government can and cannot do in secret, Dixon," Sloane said in a light manner that Sydney would have suspected was a joke if she knew him to have a sense of humor.

"Good point," Weiss eagerly agreed, causing Sydney to want to bury her head in her hands. By the look on her face, Nadia did as well.

Sloane ignored the blatant brownnosing and continued. "On the bright side, we were able to obtain positive confirmation that Malcolm Norwood was behind the break in at the FBI lab in Washington. He also confirmed, in his own roundabout way, that there was only one person who purchased that information."

"Unfortunately that buyer's already gone and put it to use," Dixon added.

"Sway," Sloane noted. "Catchy name for what could quickly become the most dangerous drug on the market."

"Do you really think it does what Norwood claimed it does?" Nadia asked.

"When I spoke with Chase, she indicated that it was entirely possible that the missing files could have been research on a similar type of drug the FBI was secretly developing," Sloane said.

Sydney did her best to ignore the implications of what Sloane was suggesting. It looked as though everyone at the table—save Sloane—was having the same thought about the government researchers overstepping their bounds. Nadia seemed to be having the hardest time reconciling herself with the idea. But, then again, she *was* the newest at this. The idea of the government secretly undermining its own positive efforts was nothing new to Sydney.

"I don't think Norwood even realized what he had," Sydney said, hoping to move the briefing forward, "or he wouldn't have been trying to sell it to Dixon. He would have held out for a bigger fish. No offense."

Dixon smiled and nodded to her, indicating that he wasn't bothered in the least over the fact that his alias didn't have a more extensive pedigree in international crime.

"A mind-control drug in the wrong hands could be devastating," Vaughn noted.

"This drug in anyone's hands could be devastating," Marshall added. "Assuming that Norwood's drink was laced with Sway, it looks like the drug takes effect immediately. As soon as it's in the system you'll do what anyone commands. *Anyone.* And it doesn't leave a trace. Nothing could be found in the glass that Dixon took from the club."

"Or in the body eighteen hours later," Weiss added. "I've just looked over Dr. Jain's complete report. There is nothing there that would indicate why Norwood pulled a gun on himself. If we didn't know anything about this drug, the only explanation would have been that the man had simply gone crazy."

"All we have is Norwood's cryptic message about 'sleeping it off,'" Dixon added. "Not that that tells us anything."

"And a search of the man's hotel room netted nothing," Sydney added, once again forced to recall the pain at the back of her head. "Although someone had done a pretty good job of searching it before and after I was attacked."

"How did she get there so quickly?" Marshall asked, as if anyone in the room had any idea. Sydney just shrugged, wanting to move on from the reminder of her failure.

"Which brings us to this woman." Sloane pressed a button and the screens in the room filled with the surveillance photo of the blonde Sydney had identified. "Felicia DeNoble, head of security for suspected international drug lord David Lowell." Sloane pressed another button on the control pad and the screen split, throwing up the image of the aforementioned drug lord. The man was not what Sydney had expected.

Sydney learned long ago not to make assumptions about people, especially in her line of business. For years, she had considered Arvin Sloane to be a noble employee of the United States government and something of a father figure, especially considering how her own father had been absent for most of her early life. Considering how that misinterpretation had turned out, she was naturally skeptical about people. Still, when she heard the words "drug lord," the image that was up on the screen was not the one that immediately popped into her head.

David Lowell was a proper-looking gentleman, with salt-and-pepper hair, lightly tanned skin, and wire-rimmed glasses. The photo on the screen was not from some grainy surveillance footage. It was a nicely posed, professionally taken portrait. It looked almost like a business photo, the kind that corporate bigwigs would take for publicity purposes. She could have almost sworn the man was wearing a thin layer of makeup on his well-moisturized skin.

"Lowell has been under investigation by the DEA for years," Jack Bristow said, taking over the brief. "He is suspected of being one of the foremost traffickers of illegal substances into the U.S. Though his involvement in the drug trade is almost common knowledge, no one has been able to find any evidence linking the man to his organization."

"Doesn't look like any drug dealer I've ever

seen," Marshall said, putting Sydney's thoughts into words. "I mean, not that I've known many drug dealers. Sure, there was that guy in college, but he was my roommate, not my supplier. I mean, not that I had a supplier. How was I supposed to know who the school would pair me with freshman year? I certainly didn't expect it to be someone that would grow marijuana in our dorm closet. Though I did learn a lot from him about the power of UV light—"

"David Lowell," Jack interrupted, "is one of Canada's more well-respected businessmen. He runs an architecture firm, is a generous contributor to politicians, and is an openhanded philanthropist. His public face often graces what one would call the society pages, though the gossip rags haven't picked up on his more unseemly pursuits. By day, he's a fine, upstanding citizen."

"And by night he's a mirror-universe Batman?" Marshall joked.

"No, he's an international drug lord," Weiss played along. "Pay attention."

Sloane was clearly not amused by the banter. "He is Canada's top developer, importer, and exporter of illegal substances. We believe that he used the money from his drug trade to build his growing public empire. In spite of his hugely successful—and legal—front company, he is still focused on drug trafficking."

"Some people never can change their ways," Sydney said offhandedly before she realized that she was talking about her own boss as well. She suspected that, subconsciously, she had been aware of that all along.

"But we're talking about run-of-the-mill drugs like E and meth, aren't we?" Vaughn asked before Sloane could take offense to Sydney's comment. "Isn't mind control a little out of his league?"

"Word on the streets is that he's been looking to expand his organization," Jack said. "We assume his own research into creating more addictive drugs led him into this area of mind-altering substances. From there he may have learned of our government's secret research, saw an opportunity, and hired Norwood to steal the files. Apparently, those files provided what he needed for his own researchers to complete their work. It would have been impossible for them to find such success with the FBI files alone. They were, as Sloane indicated, incomplete."

"Too bad Lowell didn't foresee that Norwood would immediately turn on him and steal the results of the research with an offer out to the first bidder," Dixon added.

"And then go and try to unknowingly sell them back to the government he stole them from in the first place," Marshall concluded. "Has an ironic sort of symmetry to it, doesn't it? I mean in a roundabout kind of way, that is."

"So now, not only do we have to get the files, but we have to get the drugs as well," Sydney summed up.

"More than that," Sloane said. "You need to bring in Lowell and destroy his lab. We can't have him leaking to our enemies the fact that the United States is researching mind-control drugs. That type of work would be in direct violation of a dozen treaties we have with other countries."

"Seems like a good reason not to do it in the first place," Nadia said. "The government probably wouldn't want our friends to know about it either. I think it's horrible that we're even talking about this."

"Be that as it may, the damage is done," Sloane said in the most soothing manner he could muster.

Sydney knew Sloane didn't like it when his people spoke their minds, but he was obviously more tolerant of his daughter. At the same time, Sydney knew that he was aware of how a discussion on the nature of government overstepping its bounds could evolve into something else entirely in this room. "Now it's time for us to undo that damage," Sloane quickly added.

"Sway could be Lowell's first foray into the biological terror market," Jack said, bringing the conversation back on track. "He's already got the infrastructure to make inroads into that area. From what we can tell about the man, his ego and ambition would imply that he's ready to move onto bigger things as well. We need to look at this as an opportunity to stop what could become a major player before he gets out of the gate."

"So where are we going?" Vaughn asked.

Sloane looked to his right. "Nadia?"

"Lowell owns property in Canada on the edge of Lake Superior," Nadia said as the screen switched to an aerial shot of what Sydney thought was an impressive-looking compound. Not much could be seen of the main house through the dense foliage, but the grounds were quite sprawling. "The DEA has made several attempts to get inside. They never made it past the front gate. We hear that the security system rivals those made by Toni Cummings, with whom we all have some familiarity."

"Conveniently, we have a relationship with her," Marshall said before realizing the way that sounded. "I mean a professional relationship. One of mutual respect. And she did make me a job offer once. Not that I'd consider taking it. Hey, wasn't she supposed to be out of business?"

Nadia waited until Marshall wound down. Sydney was thankful for the interruption. She wasn't sure how Sloane had taken Nadia's comment about knowing Cummings personally. Nadia had never actually forged a personal relationship with the woman. Cummings had been the one who prepared the system that had ultimately been installed in Sloane's Kyoto home, the same one where he had forced Nadia to use the Rambaldi elixir to draw a map to his still unclear endgame.

"The system is believed to be on par with Cummings's work," Nadia clarified, "but it's actually the creation of Lowell's security chief, Felicia DeNoble."

"We are going to use her to get to him," Sloane

said, "just like we did with Toni Cummings."

Sydney didn't bother to remind him that he really had nothing to do with the CIA's prior dealings with Cummings, or the fact that they had once used her to get to *him*. "You're suggesting we find Felicia, bring her in, and make her an offer to avoid prosecution in exchange for giving us the way into Lowell's compound?"

"And telling us where the lab is located," Sloane added.

Sydney was immediately skeptical. This was the woman who had managed to take Sydney down in a matter of seconds. She didn't think it would be that easy to approach the woman, much less bring her over to their side. But Sydney wasn't the only skeptic in the room.

"I don't think that's going to work," Weiss said. Sydney couldn't help but notice that even Weiss looked surprised by the fact that he had just disagreed with Sloane.

CHAPTER 5

"Excuse me?" Sloane asked, more than a little taken aback.

"I mean, I'm sorry, sir, but I don't think that plan is the best way to proceed," Weiss said. He couldn't believe he had just blurted out his thoughts like that, but now he was committed. He looked over at Vaughn, who seemed to be silently willing him to calm down. If only he could.

"Go on," Sloane prodded. He did not look happy.

"It said in the files Nadia and I went through

that Felicia has been involved with her boss for years. Personally involved, that is. I don't think she'd turn on him that easily," Weiss said.

"Everyone has her price," Sloane said. "Trust me. I have witnessed firsthand even the most loyal of associates willing to turn on one another."

Weiss knew better than to point out that he had witnessed Sloane turn on his associates on more than one occasion as well. But that didn't mean that everyone was like him. "That's the point," Weiss said instead. "You can't think of the two of them as *associates*. Based on everything we found in the files, it's much more serious than that. Lowell has effectively made her his partner, in business and in life. He's entrusted her with pretty much the keys to the kingdom if anything happens to him. I don't think they have the kind of relationship that can be broken so easily."

"Correct me if I'm wrong," Sloane said, "but you do not know either of these people personally?"

"Well . . . no."

"Then how is it you claim to know the depth of their relationship?" Sloane asked in a manner that indicated he wasn't looking for an answer. "I think, Mr. Weiss, that you are romanticizing the situation."

"I agree that going after Felicia could be risky," Nadia jumped in, much to Weiss's relief, and Sloane's noticeable chagrin. "If Lowell catches on to the fact that we've got Felicia, he could go into hiding. Considering that the DEA couldn't find anything substantive on him for this long, I don't think we'll do much better when he has reason to believe we're coming for him. In the time it would take us to turn Felicia against Lowell, he could have plenty of chances to close up shop and disappear."

"Taking the files and Sway with him," Weiss said.

"It doesn't strike me that a man with Lowell's ego would disappear from the public eye so readily," Sloane said.

"But taking his money and resources into account, a disappearing act wouldn't be much of a problem," Sydney added. Weiss was additionally thankful for that little comment. Though Sloane would listen to his daughter's opinion, Sydney and Jack were the people in the room that he would go to for a final judgment.

Sloane sat quietly for a moment. Weiss feared that he had already said too much. He shouldn't have bothered trying to remind Sloane that Lowell could take the files and the drug with him wherever he went. That much was obvious. *Should have just let Nadia and Sydney have the last words and leave it at that,* Weiss thought. As much as Sloane would listen to them, he invariably wouldn't want to look like he was taking direction from Weiss, would he?

Finally, Sloane turned to him. "What do you suggest?"

Weiss wasn't sure he had heard Sloane correctly. He hadn't anticipated being put on the spot so quickly. "Um . . . well . . . as far as Lowell knows, Malcolm Norwood was going to sell Sway to the first buyer that came along. In this case it was Dixon. I say we let that work for us. Have Dixon approach Lowell and make an offer for his entire stock."

"How do you propose getting around the DEA?" Jack asked. "If Lowell is under constant surveillance, it's going to be difficult to make the approach without attracting unwanted attention."

Although his question showed he was skeptical, Jack sounded like he was warming to the idea. Weiss knew that if he could get Jack Bristow on his side as well, the mission was practically sold. Thankfully, Weiss had already considered the complication Jack had mentioned. "We bring the DEA in on the deal. Work up a cover story. Say we're from another agency—Homeland Security, for instance—tracking Lowell, and looking to combine resources."

"The DEA isn't going to like anyone interfering with their business," Sloane said.

"Tough," Weiss said, and instantly regretted it. The look on Sloane's face made him regret it a little more. "I mean . . . tough for them. We're Homeland Security, after all. They'll fall in line. For the greater good and what not. It's all in how we make our approach."

"And how do you suggest we do that?" Sloane asked.

"Straightforward," Weiss said. "No games. Just lay it out on the line for them. Tell them Lowell is into bigger things and we need to stop him before his business affects national security."

"While we're lying about who we are and what we really want?" Marshall cut in.

"It shouldn't be hard to pull off," Weiss said.

"I'm reluctant to use Homeland Security as a cover for our operations," Sloane said. "It could lead to unwanted complications. At the same time it would be the most logical alias to pursue. Considering it seems like this course of action holds the majority appeal, maybe we should make an attempt at this route first. Never let it be said that I am not open to suggestions."

Weiss couldn't help but notice that Sloane seemed to be directing that line to Nadia. It was almost like he wanted her to know the only reason he was going along with this idea was because of her. Weiss was so caught up in the father-daughter dynamic that he nearly missed it when Sloane said, "You will head up the mission."

Suddenly Weiss realized that all eyes—including Sloane's—were on him. "I'm sorry, what?"

"I said, you will head up this mission," Sloane repeated, but it still didn't make any sense.

This was the last thing that Weiss had expected. "But Dixon—"

"Cannot risk making contact with the DEA while trying to get close to Lowell," Sloane replied. "It could compromise his cover. No. We need someone else to oversee the operation and coordinate the second team."

"Second team?" Weiss asked. Nothing in his plan had called for multiple ops.

"As soon as we get the information on the lab that created this drug, we are going to need to move in," Sloane said. "We can't just send in the CIA proper. The files are too highly classified. We need to handle this ourselves, destroy everything in existence regarding this drug and any ties it may have to the U.S. government. And we need to do it *before* it gets out on the market. I want the second team to be ready to go in at a moment's notice."

Weiss knew he should have thought of that. They'd need to move in as soon as they got the information on the lab from Lowell. Dixon couldn't do both at the same time, especially since the lab could be anywhere in the world.

"Okay," Weiss said. "I'd suggest Nadia joins Dixon and me in Canada as the first team, and Vaughn and Sydney can hold back to infiltrate the lab once we have the location."

"I'd prefer Sydney be on your team," Sloane said without even bothering to give the matter a moment of thought.

"But Felicia might recognize her from the club," Weiss said, "or from when they fought."

"Sydney was deeply made-up during the time," Sloane reminded him. "It's doubtful she would be recognized. And even if Felicia does realize Sydney was the one she fought, that could work in our favor," Sloane said. "I think the three of you would make a good team for this mission."

Weiss suspected that it was more likely that Sloane wanted his two more highly trained agents working on it, in case the plan got screwed up. *Or, more likely, he thinks* I'll *screw it up,* Weiss thought darkly. Then again, Weiss wondered if this was just Sloane's way of keeping Nadia away from him. Sloane certainly wasn't above that kind of manipulation—tying personal issues into work situations was not a foreign concept to the man.

"Work up the full mission op," Sloane instructed, "and submit it for my approval."

"Yes, sir . . . I mean, yes, Mr. Sloane."

"Thank you," Sloane said, dismissing the team.

As everyone but Vaughn filed out, Weiss stayed behind wondering what he had just gotten himself into.

"Good job there, buddy," Vaughn said with a pat on Weiss's shoulder once the room was empty.

"You were the one who told me to stand up for myself," Weiss said. "That's what Jack supposedly likes about you."

"Yeah," Vaughn said, "but Jack usually prefers it when I stand up for myself on things that he agrees with. He's not too happy when I go against him. Much like Sloane didn't appreciate it here. Yep. You really scored some points with your new girlfriend's father today."

"Thanks," Weiss said. "You're a load of help."

CHAPTER 6

Weiss finally found the strength to get up from his seat. The mission brief hadn't gone the way he had expected. Being put in charge of the op wasn't the result he had intended when he foolishly voiced his opinion. He was just looking to get on Sloane's good side. That, and he actually believed that he was right. Approaching Felicia DeNoble would have blown up in their faces. He had just wanted to point out to Sloane that there may have been a flaw in his plan and offer an alternative suggestion. He hadn't expected the man would actually take him seriously.

"Why are you so nervous? You've run ops before," Vaughn asked as they left the conference room.

"Not for Sloane," Weiss said. "I haven't worked with the man all that much over the years. *Against* him, yes, but not for him. I don't have the same insight into him as you have, or certainly, Syd. I don't know what to expect if, say, I fail at this."

"He will kill you," Vaughn said, straight-faced.

For the briefest of moments Weiss believed his friend. But then reality set in. "I'm overreacting, aren't I?"

"You're freaking out," Vaughn said.

"Can you blame me?" Weiss asked. "The man isn't exactly known for his tolerance of failure."

"Why do you keep thinking you're automatically going to fail?" Vaughn asked. "It's a straightforward mission. Get in. Get the information. Pass it along. That's all you have to do. Heck, you don't even have to do that. Sydney and Dixon are doing all the heaving lifting. You'll hardly have any chances to botch the mission."

"Thanks for the vote of confidence," Weiss said as they walked through the hall. He felt like everyone on the support staff was staring at him, wondering if he was going to mess it up. Weiss knew it was just paranoia. There was no way anyone outside the conference room knew what had just transpired. Still, he did suffer from a very active imagination. "Now let's imagine the many ways it can all go wrong," he said.

"It will with that attitude," Vaughn said. "You've got to stop letting Sloane get to you."

"You don't think . . ."

"What?"

Weiss didn't want to say it, because to say it would put it out there. And if he put it out there, it could be true. And if it was true, well, he didn't want to even think about it. Suddenly Weiss felt like he was back in high school trying to work up the nerve to ask Suzie Jacobson to the prom, all the while knowing her father, Reverend Jacobson, would never allow it. He really thought he had outgrown this stuff when he had graduated from college. But no, the only thing that seemed to have changed over the years was that now he was wearing better clothes.

Finally he resigned himself to the fact that speaking it aloud wouldn't make it any more or less true. "You don't think Sloane could be setting me up to fail?"

Vaughn didn't answer for a moment, which just confirmed what Weiss was thinking as far as he was concerned.

"Say something!" Weiss pled.

"You're insane," Vaughn replied. "Absolutely certifiable."

"You don't think Arvin Sloane likes to manipulate people like this?" Weiss asked.

"I *know* Arvin Sloane is a master of manipulation," Vaughn said way too loudly, in Weiss's opinion. "Which is exactly why this kind of thing is entirely beneath him. I don't think he would even consider wasting his time on it. And I don't see why you're wasting your time worrying about it."

"You're right," Weiss said. "I'm clearly not important enough for him to worry about—even though Nadia is his only daughter and he's trying like the devil to get a relationship going with her. Tell you what, I'll let this go as soon as you stop letting Jack get to you." Feeling like he had made his point, Weiss split off from Vaughn to start gearing up for his mission.

Weiss knew that Vaughn had made some real sense, but there was no telling that to the voice in the back of his mind. For some reason, that pipsqueak of a voice was insisting that this mission would make or break his working relationship with Sloane as well as his growing personal relationship with Nadia. Again, he knew it was an idiotic and juvenile way to think, but he couldn't stop himself. He preferred to blame it on the damned little voice and delegate any responsibility for future childish behavior to it all the same.

"Hey there, Marshall, got a minute?" Weiss asked as he entered the cluttered workroom of the head of op tech engineering. Shelves lined the walls from floor to ceiling, displaying various pieces of technology with their innards exposed. On the surface it seemed like a disorganized mess, but Weiss had come to learn that Marshall had his own way of organizing things. There was no doubt Marshall could find anything that anyone would ever need with only a moment's notice.

"Sure, what do you need?" Marshall replied as he put down a flashlight he was working on. Weiss could only guess what secondary purpose he was altering the device for. He imagined it would make a good weapon, or maybe a flare gun.

"What have you got for me?" Weiss asked.

"A genius-level IQ and too much free time,"

Marshall replied. "Well, except that last part. I don't really have *any* free time since Mitchell was born. Not that I'm complaining or anything. I love the little guy. Still . . . every now and then . . . but that's not your problem, is it?"

"I mean for the mission," Weiss prodded politely. Though he normally would be happy to talk about any problems the new father may be having, Weiss had other things on his mind at the moment.

"Well, that's a very good question," Marshall said as he slid his chair across the room to his storage locker. He punched a ridiculously long code number into the keypad lock and opened the metal double doors. Inside the locker looked like a cross between a cosmetics counter, a junk drawer, and, surprisingly enough, an actual gun cabinet. "What do you need?"

"Well . . . ," Weiss said, stalling, as he looked over the contents. The only things that he recognized were the guns and he had no way to know if they were indeed actual weapons just based on appearance, given Marshall's method of developing items with secondary purposes. Weiss could easily see the guy creating a gun that was really a hair dryer. Not that Weiss could imagine a mission-related purpose for a gun that doubled as a hair care product. Then again, he could never come up with half the things Marshall had swimming around in his brain. "Let's go back to the original question," Weiss said, giving up on figuring out what everything in front of him did. "What have you got?"

Marshall looked very pleased with himself. This was a common expression for the guy as far as Weiss could tell. Marshall tended to vacillate between nervous excitement and self-satisfied pride, with a dash of childlike wonder thrown in from time to time. "I've got anything you could possibly need for anything you could possibly encounter. Okay, that's an exaggeration, but I'm feeling particularly good today. Carrie and I are finally getting a parents' night out tonight. Do you know when the last time I had a parents' night out was? I tell ya, I don't think we've *ever* had a parents' night out before. And I could really use a parents' night out, if you know what I mean."

"Rarely," Weiss joked. "The mission?"

"Yes!" Marshall dug into the cabinet. "Since we don't have a clue what kind of security to expect, we're going to need one of these." He handed Weiss an electronic keychain.

"We get a car on this mission?" Weiss asked. "How very Q of you. I mean the Bond Q, not the *Star Trek* one."

"Yeah," Marshall said dryly. "Never heard that one before."

Okay, there's definitely something wrong when Marshall Flinkman, of all people, is making fun of me, Weiss thought.

"Now, you press that alarm button—*don't press it now!*—but when you do press it you'll activate a signal jammer. Should shut down any remote electrical system or video surveillance for a full minute."

"Great," Weiss said. "What else?"

"I'm thinking we should stick to the basics, since we don't know much about this compound," Marshall said as he pulled items from the shelves. "Couple minicameras, standard communications system, maybe a listening device for long-distance eavesdropping. It won't work on Lowell's huge compound, but it could come in handy elsewhere—though I don't really know if any of this stuff will work."

"Don't be so hard on yourself," Weiss said. "Your toys never failed us before."

Marshall looked like Weiss had just spit in his face. "My *toys* aren't the problem," he said. "It's Lowell's compound. From what I read in those classified DEA files you forwarded earlier, the reason no one's been able to get anything on the drug lord guy is because his place seems to be protected by its own electronics-jamming signal. Nothing's been able to penetrate it."

"Well, if anyone can build something that can break through it, that person would be you."

"Thank you," Marshall said. "I know you're just buttering me up because you want something else from me, but I'll take a compliment where I can get it."

Weiss was impressed by how well Marshall could read him. And maybe a little disappointed in his own lack of powers of persuasion as well. "How about anything that could counteract this Sway drug?"

"Ipecac?" Marshall suggested. "You know, to induce—"

"I know what ipecac is used for," Weiss said. "I was thinking something more along the lines of an antidote."

"Can't make an antidote when I don't know the drug," Marshall said. "Dr. Jain's information was pretty useless. But maybe we can hook you up with some truth-type serum. It won't make anyone do what Sway can, but it could come in handy in some yet unseen way. You never know."

"That's good," Weiss said. "And maybe a non-lethal weapon. A tranq gun or something like that, just in case things get out of hand."

"I'll put together a kit," Marshall said. "A little pharmacy in a box to handle anything you might come across."

Weiss nodded in appreciation as he took one last look at the cabinet. He knew that he was probably overlooking something that he would need. At the same time, he also knew that he couldn't anticipate everything that could possibly go wrong on the mission. Part of him wanted to tell Marshall to box up the entire locker. He knew that was a ridiculous precaution, but he still wanted to do it. Of course, he could only imagine Arvin Sloane's reaction if he walked out of here with a half-dozen trunks full of gadgets and weapons. Nope. He'd just have to make due with what he got.

"Thanks, Marshall," Weiss said. "This should be everything."

He could only hope that it was. Weiss would have felt much more confident if he could only have gotten that nagging suspicion about Sloane's true motivation for charging him with this mission out of the back of his mind.

"I think my father put Eric in charge of this operation as some kind of test," Nadia said. "Like a challenge for Eric to prove himself as being worthy of me or something like that. Am I being crazy?"

Sydney sipped her coffee as she considered her answer. She had suspected the conversation was coming when Nadia had suggested they leave the APO bunker to get some coffee. The little coffee shop outside the subway station that served as the cover for APO's base of operations was quickly becoming a place where the sisters would go to have their more private conversations. Sydney was pretty sure that APO headquarters wasn't bugged like the old SD-6 offices had been, but she figured it didn't hurt to play the odds.

They were sitting at a table inside the cozy place. Los Angeles was experiencing one of its rarest of all weather phenomena: a rainy day. Luckily most Angelinos preferred not to venture out in even a light drizzle, so the place was a bit emptier than normal. There were only a few aspiring writers working on their laptops and enjoying the free wi-fi connection around them. Nadia had commandeered a small table with two cushiony leather chairs while Sydney procured the coffee.

"So you think so too?" Nadia finally asked when it was clear that no answer was forthcoming.

"Let's just say I wouldn't put it past him," Sydney said. "But you can't start playing this game."

"What game?"

"The one where you start second-guessing everything Sloane does," Sydney said. "It could seriously drive you insane."

"But does he really think he's going to win my affection this way?" Nadia asked.

"I don't think he knows what to think," Sydney said. "You have to understand, Nadia, this is all new territory for him. I've never seen him like this before."

"Like what?"

"Afraid," Sydney replied without having to think about it. "You scare him. He doesn't know how to be around you."

"Wow," Nadia said. "I never expected you to be so understanding about him."

"Years of practice delving into his mindset," Sydney replied. "Besides, I'm not doing this for his benefit. I'm doing this for yours."

This time, they both sat in silence for a moment while they sipped their coffee to avoid conversation.

"Look," Sydney eventually said. "You like Weiss, right?"

Nadia smiled coyly.

"I thought so," Sydney said. "This thing you two have, it's still new. Just enjoy it. Don't worry about what your father might say or do to get in the way. Ignore it—or else you'll be spending all your time apologizing for your father."

"Sounds like you're speaking from experience," Nadia said.

This time it was Sydney's turn to flash a coy smile. Her sister had no idea the kinds of games Sydney had been forced to play with her father and Vaughn. But now was not the time to go into all that. Nadia needed to build her relationships on her own. This wasn't the time to taint them with Sydney's experiences, especially since she had gotten over most of her issues with her father.

Of course that naturally allowed Sydney's mind

to drift to thoughts of Vaughn's father. The man had supposedly died many years ago, making that relationship open to debate in her opinion. After all that Vaughn had been through recently to determine whether his father was still alive, Sydney couldn't help but wonder if everyone she knew had some lingering father issues. And that, even more naturally, led her mind to the one place she didn't want it to go.

"What?" Nadia asked.

"What, what?" Sydney replied.

"Something's wrong," Nadia said, showing an acute awareness for her sister's mood. Considering they had only really known each other for a few months, it could spark an interesting debate on the subject of nature versus nurture with regard to family bonds. But that was a conversation for another time.

"No," Sydney said. "It's nothing, really. It's stupid."

"This seems to be the day for stupid," Nadia said. "I told you mine. You tell me yours."

"But it really—"

"Sydney."

"Okay," Sydney said. "All this talk about parents

and relationships . . . I still haven't met Vaughn's mother."

Nadia did her best to hide her wide-eyed surprise. Unfortunately her best wasn't good enough to fool Sydney's acute ability to read body language. "Never?" Nadia asked.

"It didn't ever seem to be the right time," Sydney said. "First we had to act like we didn't have feelings for each other when I was working under him infiltrating SD-6. Then, once we finally got together, there was never a moment's peace. Then I had two years of my life stolen. He married Lauren—"

"She's been gone a while now," Nadia said gently.

"But his mother didn't know he had married a two-faced traitor to our country," Sydney said without bothering to conceal the venom in her voice. "I'm not even sure what he told his mom about her and her death, if she even knows that Lauren is, in fact, dead. I think it's a little too soon for him to start bringing around the new woman in his life. Besides, I'm not even sure where he and I are at the moment."

"I think that asking him to meet his mother might be a good way to jump-start that particular discussion," Nadia said.

"You're a big help," Sydney said, but she couldn't hold back the laughter.

"I'm just saying that I shouldn't be the only one that has to play these silly games," Nadia said.

Sydney took another sip of her coffee. She knew Nadia was right. It wouldn't hurt to bring up the idea. The worst Vaughn could say was that he didn't think now was the right time. At least the issue would be out in the open then. But that wasn't really the problem. The real issue was simple. It was the same thing that most women worried about in their relationships at one time or another.

What would Vaughn's mother think of her when they did meet?

On the bright side, she thought, *my head is now hurting for another reason entirely.*

CHAPTER 7

SCARBOROUGH, ONTARIO
OUTSIDE TORONTO

Sydney bit into the miniquiche and immediately regretted it. With so many on-the-job hazards, she really hated when she had to add hors d'oeuvres to the list. "Phoenix to Outrigger," she said into the hidden microphone in her necklace. "Beware the miniquiche. Consider yourself warned."

"Noted," Dixon answered back. "I'll stick to the crab puffs."

"There are crab puffs?" Sydney asked excitedly. They had arrived ahead of schedule for the event and she hadn't had time for lunch. Considering the event was already running behind schedule, there was no reason she couldn't get in a little on-the-job snacking. It was part of her cover, after all.

Though the Guild of All Arts was now a public park, part of the area had been blocked off for a private fund-raising garden party. They had lucked out and chosen a beautiful afternoon for the event. The planners were hoping to restore the area to its original beauty with the help of concerned—and notable—citizens. APO records indicated that David Lowell was a major contributor to the cause and was supposed to receive an award stating as much. Sidney assumed that, like so many other crime figures, he probably liked to cultivate a benevolent public face to help hide his illegal activities. From what she had learned so far about the man, he also seemed to enjoy playing up his public persona in the press and related venues. She quickly added "likes making an entrance" to her list of things she had concluded about him, as he was running on the fashionably late side for the event. Naturally the guests were all abuzz, wondering when the guest of honor would arrive. It was *positively* the talk of the hors d'oeuvres table.

"Shows a lack of class, if you ask me," an elderly

lady in an unfortunate outfit to Sydney's right said. At first, Sydney thought the woman had been addressing the man beside her, who Sydney assumed was her husband. But when Sydney caught the woman looking directly at her awaiting a response, she realized she was mistaken. Sydney dropped the miniquiche back onto her plate and turned to the woman. "I'm sorry?" she asked.

"David Lowell," the woman exclaimed. "Keeping us all waiting like this. Don't get me wrong, the man has done some wonderful things for the community—absolutely wonderful—but what makes him think we have all day to wait around for him?"

"Maybe he just got tied up," Sydney said, looking for a way to extract herself from the conversation.

"Oh, no, he just wants to make sure everyone's here when he makes his grand entrance," she said. "He'll probably come riding up in a horse-drawn carriage. Never saw a bigger show-off in my life." The woman then quickly added, "Bless his heart."

"Bless his heart, indeed," Sydney said with a nod as she excused herself. Annoying though the proper people of Scarborough seemed, at least she didn't have to scream over the driving beat of techno on this mission. A nice little string quartet was providing the music for the afternoon. If she hadn't been working, Sydney would have thoroughly enjoyed the relaxing event.

Sydney took in the surroundings. She had opted against any wig or eccentricities for her current alias. The bump on her head was no longer tender, but she didn't want to risk aggravating it by keeping a wig on it all afternoon. Besides, the garden party atmosphere was simpler and more subdued than most of the wigs in her collection of disguises would be appropriate for. As such, she let her long brown hair hang loose and wore a simple sundress.

It was unseasonably warm in Toronto for the fall and she was dressing to blend in, for a change. In her opinion, Sydney thought that she successfully managed to match the style of the few young women in the place. The fact that most of the guests seemed to be sixty and over stood out in stark contrast to the last place she had gone undercover. She didn't even bother to worry about what it meant that she felt far more comfortable with this crowd than with the kids.

Dixon, meanwhile, had on a crisp light gray

linen suit that looked quite nice against his dark skin. For the moment they were working two sides of the party, not wanting to appear like they were together for fear of scaring Lowell off before they could make an offer. There was no use in letting him think numerous people were already on to Sway.

"I've got Felicia," Dixon said. "At the entrance."

Sydney turned her attention to the white archway through which guests were entering the party. The design of the event was both simple and impractical at the same time. The organizers had placed potted plants in and among the existing sculptures and gardens to section off the party from the public. This left only one way in and out of the event, which bothered Sydney from a practical standpoint if something were to go wrong when they approached Lowell.

"Any sign of Lowell?" Weiss asked over the comm.

"Negative," Sydney replied. Felicia, who indeed was blond, was entering the party alone. "It looks like she's doing a security sweep."

To anyone else it probably would have just seemed like Felicia was circulating along with the hors d'oeuvres, but Sydney had enough experience in surveillance to know when someone was sweeping a room—or in this case, a garden party.

"Taking up an alternate position," Dixon noted. Sydney watched as he slipped back behind a rather large sculpture to keep himself hidden from Felicia. If the security chief saw the man who had been meeting with Norwood in New York, there was no way that Lowell would be coming in. Sydney considered hiding herself, but she had been under a wig and heavy makeup at Cube. There was little chance that Felicia would recognize the person she had attacked in New York at a Canadian garden party. Still, Sydney avoided giving the woman a chance to get a good look at her face.

Sydney busied herself with the remains of her bitter miniquiche and kept an eye on Felicia at the same time. The woman's gaze passed Sydney quickly, leaving her to think that she was in the clear. But a moment later, Felicia's eyes returned to Sydney. There seemed to be a look of recognition mixed with uncertainty.

Sydney turned away from Felicia under the pretense of throwing away her food. "I think I've been made," she said into the comm.

"Confirmed," Dixon said. "She's got you in her sights, Phoenix."

"She recognizes you?" Weiss asked over the comm.

"Probably not," Dixon said. "But she does look suspicious. I don't know if she'll clear the way for Lowell."

"Okay," Weiss said quickly. "Time for a new plan. Syd, go make contact with Felicia and get her to bring in Lowell."

"Okay," Sydney said. She turned back to Felicia and saw that the woman was still looking at her, without trying to look like she was looking. Sydney didn't bother with the pretense and strolled right up to Felicia to say hello.

"Seems like we've both come a long way since our days as cocktail waitresses for the young and obnoxious," Sydney said as she reached the woman. A flash of realization crossed Felicia's face as her hand slid toward her purse and, presumably, her gun. "There's no need for that," Sydney said lightly. "I'm just here to reminisce, not seek retribution, even though that was quite a bump you gave me. Haven't been able to do a thing with my hair since."

"You don't seem worse for the wear," Felicia said.

"Can't say the same thing about our mutual friend, Mr. Norwood."

"That man was no friend of mine," Felicia replied, flipping her hair carelessly and continuing to scan the party at the same time. Sydney could tell that the woman had just locked her eyes on Dixon.

"That's obvious in hindsight," Sydney said. "But what I want to know is how did you get into his hotel room so quickly?"

"I'm just good at what I do," Felicia replied. "Now, can we cut the banter and get to you telling me what you want?"

"It's not what I want so much as what my boss wants," Sydney said. She nodded her head back over her shoulder in Dixon's direction and followed Felicia's eyes as they returned to the back of the garden party. Dixon raised his glass of champagne and flashed a smile when Felicia's eyes fell on him. She nodded in response.

"How did you find me?" Felicia asked.

"Well, I think we both know it's not *you* we're looking for," Sydney said offhandedly. "Now, just so you know, we do realize that Mr. Norwood was not representing your employer in any way. That doesn't matter to us. We have no ties—or *had* no ties—to Mr. Norwood beyond the product he was trying to sell us.

"He had no right to make that offer," Felicia said. "He did not own the product."

"Yes," Sydney said. "We have since been made aware of that. But it doesn't lessen our interest any. We would still like to speak to Mr. Lowell about it. My employer can be a very generous man."

"I'm not sure Mr. Lowell is in the market to sell at the moment," Felicia said.

Sydney nodded. "That's understandable. He needs to figure out what he's got, what kind of doors this could open for him. . . . There's a lot at stake here. My employer just wants to have a chance to make the opening bid—maybe with an option to match any top offer that comes in."

"It's tempting," Felicia said. "But I'm afraid we're not here for business today. Maybe you noticed when you came in that this event was set up to honor Mr. Lowell for his philanthropic work."

"Any reason for a fund-raiser, I guess," Sydney said with an exaggerated shrug. "We've already made our contribution at the door. We're planning on sticking around to see what it gets us."

"I will bring the idea to Mr. Lowell's attention," Felicia said. "In the meantime, feel free to enjoy the afternoon and watch him receive his award."

"Sounds lovely," Sydney said as she leaned in. "A word of warning though. Steer clear of the miniquiches. But I hear the crab puffs are *delish.*"

Felicia flashed an almost genuine smile as her eyes made one last sweep of the grounds before she turned and headed out of the party. Hopefully she would be returning with her boss and not slipping away.

"Well, we've made contact," Sydney said as she went to join Dixon.

"I've got her now," Weiss said over the comm. "I can see why Lowell likes to mix business and pleasure."

"Don't we all," Sydney mumbled offhandedly. In fact Sydney and her coworkers' personal lives seemed to be intermingled past the point of logic sometimes, as far as she was concerned.

"Do you think she calls him Mr. Lowell in private?" Weiss asked over the comm. "Because that would just be wrong in their more intimate moments."

"Personally, I'd prefer not to think about their more intimate moments," Sydney said as Dixon came over and handed her one of the treats she had already heard so much about.

"Point taken," Weiss agreed. "Well, I'm off to do my part. Enjoy your boring speeches and save me a crab puff."

"Sorry," Sydney said as she bit into the tasty delicacy and immediately understood what Dixon had been raving about, "but you're on your own."

Weiss chuckled softly as he listened to Sydney enjoying her snack and wished that the microphone wasn't so close to her mouth. "I've got Lowell," he said as he tracked Felicia moving toward a row of cars parked down the road. He mentally kicked himself for missing her entrance earlier. Apparently the woman was very good at making herself appear inconspicuous. Even so, Weiss was glad that Sloane wasn't looking over his shoulder to see that particular slip-up.

David Lowell was in a small Lexus convertible with the top up, talking on his cell phone, when Felicia tapped on the window. Weiss gave the guy points for immediately ending the call and getting out of the car. Very few important businessmen were able to end a call so suddenly. Then again, the guy could have been talking to his mother and thought that his waiting audience took precedence.

Lowell was taller than Weiss had imagined. Standing beside the small car added to the illusion that he was a considerably imposing figure. This was all offset by the pleasant, innocent look on his face. Even at a distance Weiss could tell that the man was a good mix of genial and intimidating that probably served him well in both his legal and illegal operations, and certainly helped him with his public image.

Lowell took Felicia's arm and together they headed for the party. It was clear that she was filling him in on the uninvited guests. It wasn't clear whether he took Dixon and Sydney's presence as a welcome opportunity or an annoyance.

Weiss didn't bother to follow the pair back to the party. Sydney and Dixon had things under control on that part of the mission. Weiss's role as lead agent on the operation called for something else—something that was going to be a lot easier than he had originally anticipated.

Weiss focused his attention on the big white utility truck at the end of the row of cars. He couldn't believe that the DEA would be so obvious. Aside from the fact that the truck stood out from its size alone, it was a telephone truck stationed in a park where the nearest phone was several blocks away.

"Going dark for a moment," Weiss said over the comm. "Try not to miss me too much."

"Not for a second," Sydney joked.

Weiss took the earpiece out of his ear and slipped it into his pocket. Before moving in, he wanted to make sure that he wasn't going to stumble across a couple of guys on their lunch break. Weiss replaced the single earpiece with a pair of earbuds and took out what was supposed to look like an iPod. Actually, it was an iPod for all intents and purposes, though Weiss was not planning on listening to tunes on what had to be the oddest selection of playlists he had ever seen. *Who puts Metallica next to selections from The Wiggles?*

The little device was among the items Weiss had borrowed from Marshall's handy little locker when he went back to double check that he hadn't overlooked anything. Or was it from when he went back for a third time? At any rate, aside from filling the MP3 player with the bizarre assortment of songs, Marshall had also turned it into a listening device, powerful enough to hear inside oversize white utility trucks, among other things.

Turning toward the truck, Weiss held up the device and aimed the port at the vehicle in question. He knew he didn't exactly look like a jogger out for an afternoon run in his suit, but he didn't look too out of place listening to tunes while standing among the nicely dressed people walking in and out of the party. No one would suspect that music wasn't coming through those earphones at the moment.

Snippets of conversation could be heard through the static. He was picking up bits and pieces of words and short phrases, but nothing that would indicate what was being discussed inside the truck. Weiss adjusted the settings as he homed in on the vehicle. It took a few seconds, but eventually he heard voices over the headphones as clearly as if they were speaking to him.

"Check out this Norwood fella they mentioned," a male voice said. "I think we've got the name in the files. And see if we can get some shots of this mystery woman and the guy she's talking to."

Two other voices confirmed that they were on task.

"Lowell's cleared the entrance," a woman's voice announced. "He's still with Felicia, but they've got to get through a gauntlet of well-wishers before they can make contact with the new players."

"And you thought nothing would happen at a silly little garden party," the man said. "You owe me ten bucks."

"Put it on my tab," the woman said.

Weiss had heard enough. He walked back to his car, dropped the iPod listening device on the front seat, locked up, and strolled over to the truck. He was doing his best to look inconspicuous in spite of the fact that the truck stuck out like a sore thumb in the middle of the park. Luckily Felicia was inside the party with Lowell, and it didn't appear that they had brought any extra security with them.

Placing the truck between him and the garden party, Weiss circled around the side and approached the back in case anyone was paying attention. He knocked on the metal doors twice and waited for a response. He figured there were a few people inside looking at one another wondering who was knocking in the middle of their surveillance operation. It took a moment for a young guy in coveralls with the local telephone company logo on the chest to open the door.

"Yeah?" the guy said. He was being careful to hold the door close to him so that Weiss could not see inside.

"Hey, I'd like a Fudgsicle, a red rocket, and a couple of those SpongeBob SquarePants bars, you know, for the kiddies," Weiss said.

The telephone guy looked annoyed. "This isn't an ice cream truck, sir. It's a utility vehicle."

"Oh," Weiss said, acting surprised. "My mistake. Didn't expect to see a utility vehicle out in the middle of a park with no utilities in sight. In that case, can I speak to your boss?" Weiss flashed a fake badge that identified him as an agent of U.S. Homeland Security.

The guy looked at the identification then quickly waved him into the truck. "Hurry up, Mr. Rayner," the guy said as he read the name of Weiss's cover alias off the identification. "We don't need you bringing any unwanted attention."

"Nope," Weiss said as he hopped into the big white truck. "Wouldn't want that, now would we?"

The inside of the utility tuck was pretty tricked

out with surveillance equipment. It was obviously a serious operation. There was nothing in the truck that Weiss hadn't seen or used before—certainly nothing compared to the kinds of things Marshall created—but it was an impressive array of technology nonetheless.

Two monitors showed video of the event from a pair of angles. One was focused on Lowell, while the other was aimed at Dixon and Sydney. Weiss knew that Sloane had wiped any images of his agents from all federal databases, so Sydney and Dixon being identified wasn't a concern. The woman sitting at the monitors had a headset on, but was only covering one ear with it. They must have had some kind of long-range listening device. It was doubtful that they could have gotten a bug on Lowell directly.

"Who do we have here?" a younger man in a suit asked as the utility guy passed Weiss's false credentials off, then headed to the front of the truck to join another uniformed guy keeping an eye on the park. "Homeland Security?"

"Figured you DEA guys might need some help since we're all far away from home in a foreign country and all," Weiss said.

"We're in *Canada*," the woman wearing the headset said. "We're across the border from home."

"Now, now, Caryn," the man said. "Mr. Rayner's just trying to be cordial because he's about to step all over our toes and interfere with our operation. Aren't you, Mr. Rayner?"

Weiss had to give the guy credit. He was sharp enough to know better and bold enough for it not to matter. Rather mature attributes for someone so young. And the kid *was* young.

"I prefer to think of it as an offer of assistance," Weiss said. "One from me to you . . . and hopefully one from you to me. It's a scratch-my-back kind of thing, uh . . . Mr. . . ?"

"Parker," the man said, holding out his hand. "Agent Trent Parker. But you probably already knew that." Weiss nodded in assent.

Agent Trent Parker looked to be the youngest lead operative Weiss had ever come across, which only served to make him feel more inadequate taking the lead on his mission. It was still a silly concern considering that this was far from the first time Weiss had overseen a mission, but it was still the first time he was doing it while reporting to Arvin Sloane.

"Samuel Rayner," Weiss said, taking the man's hand without bothering to confirm or deny how much he knew about the operation, "as you've probably noted from my ID. But you can call me Sam . . . Sammy . . . or any derivation thereof."

"So, what's the problem, Sammy?" Parker said as he leaned against the surveillance console. Weiss couldn't tell if the guy was really that relaxed or if he was putting up a front to hide how annoyed he was. Weiss wouldn't blame Parker if he were feeling put out. He didn't like it when other agencies tried to interfere with his work—especially considering that other agencies didn't know that his work was *unofficially* sanctioned by the government.

"David Lowell," Weiss said.

Parker nodded. "Kind of figured. But what's our boy gone and done that's got Homeland Security interested?"

"Well, now that's the problem," Weiss said. "I'm not really at liberty to say much for the time being. But I will tell you that we've recently gotten some intel that suggests he's dabbling in somewhat larger enterprises of late."

Parker exchanged a glance with the woman at the surveillance monitors. "Can't say we're surprised," he said. "We've been hearing the buzz. Nothing substantial, but Lowell's been a lot happier lately, bordering on ecstatic. Homeland Security, huh? Lowell's got big dreams and all, but I don't think there's anything that needs to be on your radar at the moment."

"The things we've been hearing suggest the opposite," Weiss said. "Brought him to our attention. I just figured we could work this together, use each other's resources and such."

"You mean pump us for information, then take all the glory when you use it to get him," the woman said.

"Caryn, was it?" Weiss asked, already knowing that he would never win this one over. He paused a moment to take in the female before him. She was a stunning African-American woman with piercing brown eyes that made it clear that she was about ready to kill him. Without realizing what he was doing, Weiss confirmed that she wasn't wearing a wedding ring, then immediately checked himself. Old habits die hard.

"Agent Hughes," she replied.

"Well, Agent Hughes," Weiss said, trying to match the attitude he was receiving, "I can assure you that I don't give a rat's ass who gets the credit for this one. I just want to make sure the bad man gets what he deserves: a nice long prison sentence—in a tiny little cell."

"We have been tracking him for years and have done extensive surveillance work to get us this far. You think you can do better?" Parker asked.

"Let's just say my people have already made some inroads," Weiss said. "Besides, it never hurts to get a fresh opinion. For instance, I would suggest that maybe using a phone company truck in the middle of a park with no payphones or telephone poles might be conspicuous."

"You're assuming that we were trying to hide," Parker said. "Every now and again I like to remind Lowell that we've got our eye on him. If he feels like he's always got to be on his toes, the pressure might make him slip."

"Good plan," Weiss said. "How's that working so far?"

Parker didn't answer, but Hughes looked like she was truly about to commit murder. Weiss made a mental note to dial it back a notch. He didn't need these people as enemies.

"Look," Weiss said, "I know how I'd feel if

someone started messing around on my turf. It's just, I've got a job to do and I don't want us getting in each other's way."

"Well now, I'm going to have to check you out before we can agree to anything," Parker said.

"Be my guest," Weiss said, knowing that any background check was going to net the DEA exactly what APO wanted them to believe about Sam Rayner and his associates. "In the meantime, I'll just ask that you don't interfere with my operation."

"And what operation is that?" Parker asked.

"We've got an approach on the two strangers," one of the guys in the front of the truck said. They had their own set of monitors up there, it seemed.

Parker looked at the screen, then back at Weiss. "Let me guess. Those are your guys?"

"Word of advice," Weiss said, "don't let the pretty lady hear you call her one of my 'guys.' Actually, don't let her hear you call her 'pretty lady,' either. But yeah, they're with me."

"You can't just walk into the middle of our operation," Hughes said, looking outraged.

"Sorry, but our mission takes precedence," Weiss said politely, trying not to anger the agent any more than he already had. "Someone will confirm that for you when you check out my creds."

"You must know we've had agents approach Lowell before," Parker said. "We've never gotten anyone on the inside. What makes you think that you're going to be more successful?"

"It's just a matter of knowing his subject of interest," Weiss said as he pulled up a chair and sat by the monitors showing Lowell and Felicia approaching Sydney and Dixon. "Here. Let's watch."

Onscreen, they saw the two couples meet off to the side of the garden party. Hughes unplugged her headset and turned up the volume so they could all listen in. From the ambient noise surrounding the conversation, Weiss was pretty much able to confirm that they were using a parabolic mike to eavesdrop instead of a good old-fashioned bug.

Time to wow the DEA folks, Weiss thought. He had utter and total faith in Sydney and Dixon's abilities to get in with Lowell. But at the same time, standing in the middle of a DEA operation with four DEA agents who presumably wouldn't mind if he failed . . . well, Weiss was feeling a bit of performance anxiety, made worse by the fact that he had no control over the current performance.

CHAPTER 8

"I'd introduce myself," David Lowell said as he approached Sydney and Dixon, "but—let's be honest—everyone here knows who I am. However, they don't know as much about me and my business interests as it appears the two of you do. So, I think the only question left is, who are you?"

"You may call me Carlton," Dixon said. "This is my associate, Morgan."

"A pleasure," Lowell said with a slight nod. "Carlton and Morgan? Would those be first names or last?"

"They would be false names," Sydney said. "So don't waste your time looking us up when we're done here. You won't find what you're looking for."

"I see you want to hold all the cards in this conversation," Lowell said through a plastered-on smile. He clearly didn't like negotiating in this manner, but he certainly wasn't going to let it show here. Sydney could see everyone at the party was surreptitiously casting glances in his direction, as he was the man of the hour. "Doesn't seem fair. You apparently already know more about me than I'd like."

"After what happened to your last associate, I prefer to play it safe," Dixon said.

"I don't know what you're talking about," Lowell said in a way that told them he knew exactly what they were talking about. Maybe Sydney was wrong, but she got a sense that he'd issued a warning that the same could happen to them if they weren't careful.

"Oh, I think you do," Sydney said, playing along and making sure he knew they meant business as well. On the surface Lowell looked amiable enough, but she didn't doubt that just beneath that cover there was a snake waiting to strike. It was best to let him know they were equally dangerous. "But we would never bother to go into more detail in such a public place. You never know when incurable gossips are listening in."

"Too true," Felicia said pointedly, confirming what Sydney had suspected. Felicia and Lowell knew they were already under surveillance.

"It's a shame," Lowell said, "because I'm dying to know how you came to know my name. I'm sure it was a fascinating bit of detective work."

"I'm afraid that this *is* the wrong place for such a private conversation," Dixon said. "It would seem the hotel we've booked is even less secure. We don't get up to Canada as often as we'd like and don't know the best places to conduct this type of business."

"That's a shame," Lowell said, clapping an arm on Dixon's shoulder and effectively diverting a gawker from coming up to say hello to him. "We do have so many things to do up here. You should really make it a point to vacation here some time."

Felicia pulled a similar move, taking Sydney by the hand to blow off the older woman that had complained about Lowell's tardiness earlier. "Did he happen to mention that he works very closely with the Bureau of Travel and Tourism?" Felicia joked.

"Another one of my pet projects," Lowell laughed falsely.

"Perhaps there is someplace we can go to speak?" Dixon said, trying to get the conversation back on track. "Someplace befitting discussions of this nature. I assure you—"

"You'll make it worth my while?" Lowell guessed blithely. "Nice to know we can always rely on a good cliché."

"But that's the point, isn't it?" Dixon asked, apparently giving in and playing along.

Sydney found Lowell's genial manner to be annoying and counterproductive to actual discourse, but it was going to be necessary to indulge him if they wanted to actually get anything done. Obviously, Dixon had come to the same conclusion.

"The clichés come in handy because they are usually so accurate," Dixon continued, "as this case demonstrates."

"I'm afraid we have a fairly full schedule," Felicia said, with an eye to the podium, where the party organizers seemed to be ready for the award presentation.

Considering Lowell's aforementioned lateness, Sydney could understand why they'd want to get started. Of course, Lowell was well aware of the fact that he was in demand. He probably felt that by stalling he made himself even more in demand. Sydney wasn't sure if that was for the benefit of the guests or of her and Dixon. Either way, she was already tired of the man. "We'd be willing to work around that schedule," Sydney offered.

"And I assure you—to use another cliché—you won't regret it," Dixon added, "if we could just find a place more suitable for conversation."

"Well, these gossips do tend to follow me around," Lowell said, offhandedly referring to the DEA agents with whom Weiss was sitting and listening to everything the quartet was saying. "Conveniently, I do know a place—a sanctuary, if you will—where I can conduct business that is more . . ."

"Lucrative?" Sydney suggested.

Lowell beamed. "I was going to say 'private,' but I like your choice of word much better. I'm afraid it is a bit of a jaunt. Can we put this off until tomorrow evening?"

"That should not be a problem," Dixon said.

"Our schedule is entirely clear until after we have a chance to speak."

"Well, then you should definitely check out the Toronto nightlife," Lowell said.

"Just stay away from those underage clubs," Felicia said jokingly. "They can be so dangerous."

"Not as dangerous as hotel rooms," Sydney replied.

"As for tomorrow," Lowell said, "you *do* have access to a plane, I hope?"

"Several," Sydney quickly replied to tantalize him with their assumed wealth.

"Wonderful," Lowell said. "My place is in Thunder Bay, just a quick hop over a couple of the lakes."

"We shall be there," Dixon said, shaking hands with Lowell.

"Looking forward to it," Felicia said as she took Sydney's hand and gave an unnecessarily tight squeeze.

Sydney was surprised that they had received an invitation to his compound so quickly. Everything in the files she had read indicated that Lowell tended to be more suspicious of people. That was supposedly why the DEA never managed to get any of their agents on the inside.

"This is perfect," Lowell said as Felicia handed him a business card that he in turn passed to Dixon. "Here is the address. Say, eight o'clock?"

"See you then," Dixon said with a nod as he and Sydney started to move off so the people gathering politely around them could have their chance to speak with the guest of honor.

Lowell gently laid a hand on Dixon's arm to stop him. "You *will* be staying around to watch me accept my award." Sydney noticed that, though it was politely phrased, it was not a question.

"I'd prefer not to draw attention to my activities," Dixon said. "You can understand how I might not want to be seen spending too much time with a fine upstanding individual such as yourself. It would do such horrible things to my reputation."

"Yes," Lowell said through a tight smile.

"Until tomorrow," Sydney said, flashing her own smile in Felicia's direction.

"Tomorrow," Felicia agreed.

Sydney and Dixon turned and walked toward the exit. "My jaw is starting to hurt from all that forced pleasantry," she said.

"And that painfully polite conversation," Dixon added. "How I long for the lowlife criminals. At least then I don't have to speak like I'm in some drawing room drama."

"Too true," Sydney said with a British accent as they left the garden party. Her mind was still on the passing servers. "Never did get that extra crab puff."

Sydney and Dixon walked to their rental car, which was parked down the road from the party. Along the way, they saw Weiss come out of the impossible-to-miss utility truck. Not wanting to risk their cover, they proceeded to ignore him as they continued toward their vehicle. Within moments, they heard his voice return over the communications system.

"We're in," Weiss said. "The DEA guys were very interested when they saw just how eager Lowell was to get you to his compound."

"It did happen a lot faster than I had expected," Sydney said as she slipped into the driver's seat.

"This could work for us," Dixon said as he got in the passenger's side of the car. "If Lowell's this eager to join the big boys, he might let down his defenses a bit, maybe move too quickly and slip up."

"That would be nice," Sydney said as she started the car. "Where are we going?"

"Rendezvousing with the lovely folks from the DEA back in Toronto," Weiss said as he got into his car three parking spots away. "They're going to wrap things up here and leave in a bit. Give us a few minutes head start so we're not caravanning it out of here. Follow me."

Sydney gave Weiss a short head start then pulled out of her spot. She caught up with him as he left the park and the two cars made their way back into Toronto. The afternoon traffic wasn't too heavy, so it only took about a half hour for them to get into the city and to the building where Weiss had arranged to meet the DEA agents.

According to Weiss, the DEA had set up permanent headquarters in Toronto across from the building where Lowell housed his legal front businesses. His architecture firm was quickly becoming one of the more notable firms in Canada. According to his financial records, he was turning quite a hefty profit off that particular enterprise. It was amazing to Sydney that his legal success wasn't enough for him. If he needed to branch out so much, why couldn't he just buy some restaurants like most bored businesspeople?

Lowell's illegal activities, on the other hand, seemed to be run exclusively out of his private home and security compound in Thunder Bay. Considering the two-hour flight between the two cities, it wasn't exactly the easiest commute. Then again, Sydney had spent far more time in the air for her job, so she had no right to judge.

What his Thunder Bay compound lacked in convenience, it more than made up for in security. Aside from its near mythical security system, the compound boasted one of the most intensive anti-surveillance initiatives this side of APO. Planes were routinely rerouted around the airspace above the compound for fear of interference with their electrical equipment. Yet inside the gates, Lowell was rumored to have an impressive communications center from which he controlled his kingdom.

"Seems to be going well so far," Weiss said as he joined Sydney and Dixon in the parking garage of the building where the DEA rented space.

"We've made contact," Dixon said straight-faced. "That was the easy part."

"I know," Weiss said. "I'm just saying, both the

DEA and Lowell seem willing to deal with us. I think that's a good sign. Come on, let's see a little optimism."

Dixon just stared at him in a way that made Sydney want to laugh. She knew Dixon was just playing with Weiss by affecting the ultraserious tone. But she certainly didn't need to rub it in. Clearly, Weiss's enthusiasm was an attempt to cover up his insecurity. The power of intimidation Sloane had over people was amazing, even from a couple of thousand miles away.

"We're doing fine," she said soothingly. "There's nothing to worry about."

Weiss didn't look relieved. "What, me worry? What could I possibly have to worry about?"

"Just have them wait for us when they get there," Agent Trent Parker said into his cell phone as they rode back to headquarters. "And be nice. We don't know what they're really up to."

Parker chose to ignore the pointed sigh from behind him as he ended the call. He leaned between the front seats of the truck where his men were sitting and checked on their progress. They were already crossing back into Toronto. A quick trip down the 404 and they'd be at headquarters, where the Homeland Security agents would be waiting for him. He had just been on the phone making arrangements for their arrival. The last thing he needed was a scene waiting for him at headquarters when he returned.

This was not how he had expected the day to turn out, although he did think that any kind of progress in this case would be good, even if it came from an external source. David Lowell was his first long-term assignment, and this was his first time leading a mission. So far, it had also been his first massive failure. They'd had a team on Lowell full-time for more than two years, and they still couldn't come up with anything that would stick. The man was always one step ahead of them, no matter what angle they tried. Maybe some new blood would help inject life into the case. He couldn't keep holding off his superiors forever.

At the same time, he had never had anyone from another agency crash a mission before. It was unsettling to say the least. And Homeland Security had to be the crashers to boot. He wasn't exactly sure what their jurisdiction was in these matters, but he didn't want to question things too much from the start. Though he hadn't been in the field as long of some of the people on his team, Parker was smart enough to know that the squeaky wheel often found himself transferred to Siberia or some equivalent. A quick call to his superior officer back in D.C. had confirmed that Homeland Security was taking over. Well, Agent Ross hadn't actually said "taking over," but the implication had been in his tone just the same.

As always, Parker didn't balk. He just accepted the call and made a mental note to have his team go over these new agents on their own. Just because Ross had given this "Sammy" guy and his team a cursory glance, didn't mean a little deeper investigation wasn't in order. If Parker was going to be working closely with them, it wouldn't hurt to know as much about them as they must know about him. A simple call back to his field office had set some of that research in motion, while alerting the office to the visitors, who would probably be getting in at any moment. Now he just had to hold things together while he learned where this new angle would lead them.

"I don't like this," Caryn Hughes finally said. Not like he couldn't have guessed her opinion by the attitude she had adopted since Agent Sammy Rayner had left the truck—or while he had still been in it. Thankfully, Dobbs and McCormack were holding judgment for the moment. Well, they may have been judging, but they weren't being vocal about it. Parker was thankful for small favors. It was hard enough running a team where he was the youngest member in the outfit. Parker didn't need a total revolt on his hands.

"I don't like it either," Parker said, making sure the guys up front could hear him clearly as well. "But I'm not going to let Lowell get away with whatever he's up to now just because you don't like to play well with others. Why don't we hold off on making any decisions until we hear these Homeland Security folks out."

"You're not seriously thinking of working with them?" Hughes asked.

"As opposed to letting them run roughshod over our operation, I think a little cooperation is exactly what's called for here," Parker said. "Besides, it's not like our superiors are going to give us a choice on this one. Ross told me everyone's onboard."

"They won't be if you put up a fight," Hughes said, "instead of just rolling over."

"That's out of line," he said, wishing he didn't sound like some stick-up-the-ass bureaucrat. He tried to lighten the mood with some playful banter. "You sound like you don't trust me."

"You, I trust," Hughes said as they bounced along a bumpy stretch of road. "I'm just not so sure about secret agents who show up out of the blue with operatives already in play. They didn't even give us a heads-up before they initiated contact with our suspect."

"I think that might be more Agent Ross's fault than theirs," Parker said. The director was notoriously lax in updating his foot soldiers on the news of the day. It wasn't like Parker could have questioned his boss on the timing. And it was easier to give his new Homeland Security friends the benefit of the doubt on that one.

"Doesn't negate the fact that this is our mission," she insisted.

"Careful," Parker warned. "You're getting a little territorial."

"Damn right I'm territorial. We don't know who the hell these people are."

Parker held up his cell phone. "The preliminary query checked out."

"That just means they're in the system," Hughes reasoned. "Doesn't mean they're really who they say they are."

"When we get back to the office, I'll have McCormack and Dobbs jump in on the full background search Stanton is already running," Parker said. "By the end of the day we'll know more about them than their own mothers do."

At that moment, Dobbs took a sharp turn, nearly throwing Parker to the floor. "Hey, watch it!" he called up to the front. "This thing isn't exactly built low to the floor. How will it look to our new friends if we're late to our first meeting because we had a rollover?"

"Sorry, boss," Dobbs called back. There was always something in the way that Dobbs said "boss" that made Parker feel like it was an insult. He couldn't help it that he was young. Dobbs was only a couple of years older than him anyway.

"And what about them not wanting to tell us what Lowell's up to?" Hughes asked, pulling Parker back to the subject at hand.

"Now you're just looking for reasons not to trust them," Parker said as he steadied himself in the truck.

"I don't need to look," she said. "They've already given us plenty of reasons right out there in the open."

Parker knew she was just frustrated and blowing off steam. Hughes liked to do that sometimes. But in the end she was a team player and would do what she was told. "So what did you expect me to do, kick the guy out of my truck and tell him to go to hell?"

"Would've been a start," she said.

"And would you have given me a recommendation when I was looking for my next job?" Parker asked more snottily than he had intended. "Because I go around treating Homeland Security like that, and all our asses will be out on the street. Caryn, if you think I've suddenly gone idiot, then maybe you should put in for a transfer. But maybe, just maybe, I've been put in charge of this mission because I know how to play the game. We may not like the game, but I am willing to play it." He knew he was being especially harsh, since Caryn's refusal to bend for anyone was the reason he was in charge and she reported to him, but Parker couldn't worry about her feelings, since she wasn't worried in the least about his.

"If these Homeland Security guys want to come along for the ride," he continued, "I'm going to let them. But at the end of the day, if they get even one iota in our way, I'm taking them down—with your help, of course."

Hughes looked at him in silence for a moment. Parker wondered if he had gone too far. He didn't usually let attitude slip into his work. He preferred a more congenial approach to things, and he wasn't sure how she would react.

Turns out, he didn't need to worry.

"Well, all right," she finally said with a smile and a nod. "Glad to hear it."

CHAPTER 9

TORONTO

Sydney, Weiss, and Dixon passed nondescript brown door after nondescript brown door. The names on the signs beside those doors seemed just as uninformative as the doors themselves. Sydney couldn't be sure if Klasky & Berkowitz; Simmons and Associates; and Perez, Pinter, and Platt were lawyers, doctors, or candlestick makers. It didn't much matter, since Weiss kept walking past them all.

When they reached a plaque that read PHARMACEUTICAL SOLUTIONS, Weiss opened the door and showed them inside. This was obviously the small company the DEA had created to headquarter the Toronto operations of the long-term surveillance op. Sydney couldn't help but appreciate the cute little joke of a name.

Inside, the reception area was just as nondescript as the hallways had been. The decor was generic with a hint of institutional and very much the way Sydney imagined every other office on the floor looked. She was standing in a basic waiting room with a couch and two chairs that matched the brown reception desk, which matched the door on the other side of the room. Aside from the basic office artwork and the potted plant, there were very little decorative touches in the room, and she was including the bland-looking receptionist who hardly looked up when they entered. Not surprisingly, she suddenly developed an immense appreciation for the design efforts that had been made in putting together APO headquarters.

Beyond the reception desk was another brown door. Sydney assumed that it led to the back offices and was hopefully more secure than it looked, because it looked pretty weak from a security perspective. Considering that all the good stuff had to be going on in the back, she imagined it wouldn't be all that easy to get inside. Of course, the DEA could just be relying on Mr. Personality at the reception desk as their security. The guy looked more like a club bouncer than an office worker.

"Can I help you?" the man asked, without cracking a smile.

"We have an appointment with Parker," Weiss said. "I'm pretty sure we beat him here."

"He's only a couple minutes out," the receptionist/bouncer said. "He called ahead to tell me you were coming. Can I get you some coffee while you wait?" The last part was added as an afterthought. Sydney assumed that someone must have spoken to him about his demeanor at some point in the not-too-distant past, because he was having a trying time playing the part of the receptionist. This was especially obvious when he finally forced a smile that looked almost as painful as any torture Sydney had experienced in the past.

Sydney, Weiss, and Dixon declined the offer of coffee and took seats while they waited. The leather on the chair Sydney chose was still pulled tight and had very little give, as if the seat was brand-new. Sydney wondered if anyone had actually sat in this waiting room before. It wasn't like DEA operatives on a secret surveillance mission were often having people come to their front company for appointments.

The three sat in silence, not wanting to give anything away to the receptionist. Even though the man behind the desk was silently working at his computer, Sydney knew that he was alert and would make note of anything they said so he could report back to his superiors after they left. For all Sydney knew, the place could be bugged, as well.

When her mind went to the possibility of bugging, a new fear popped up. If Lowell knew the DEA team was watching him, what would stop him from watching the DEA team? If this office was under surveillance by Lowell, they could have already blown their cover. Sydney just had to trust that Agent Parker and his team knew what they were doing, as the damage would already have been done.

Sydney got her wandering thoughts under control as the DEA team arrived. Two of the four members of the team barely acknowledged her presence as they nodded hello to the burly receptionist and made their way through the security door. A man and a woman remained in the lobby as Sydney, Weiss, and Dixon stood for introductions.

Weiss took care of the formalities, introducing Sydney as Agent Sylvia Newton and Dixon as Agent Chris Soto. Considering it was too risky to use their real names on this mission, Marshall had provided them all with fake agent names so when Agent Parker ran a background search on Homeland Security agents, he would come up with something. Add to that the aliases they had provided Lowell—namely Carlton and Morgan—and they were going to have to work a cover alias within an alias on this mission. Dual aliases were nothing new to the former double agent. It just made things more interesting as far as Sydney was concerned.

"Why don't we take this little get together inside," Parker said as he led them to the back offices. "Jeff did offer you all some coffee, right?"

Weiss nodded. "We're fine."

"Good call," Parker said once the outer door was shut. "Jeff's coffee is about the consistency of a mud bath. But not nearly as therapeutic." He led them down a hall past four closed doors, which suggested that the DEA team consisted of the five people Sydney had already met. That seemed about right to her for the mission. She wondered if anyone had switched out since the beginning. If the DEA kept the same people on from the start of the mission, with nothing to show for it after a couple of years, maybe it was time to shake things up a bit. She only hoped that she wasn't going to be the one doing the shaking.

"Here we go," Parker said as he ushered them into a small conference room with large glass windows and a telescope aimed at the building across the street. A variety of listening devices were sitting on shelves on the side wall, along with video equipment and monitors. This conference room was probably the center of their operation.

"Thanks," Weiss said. "You've been pretty accommodating. We appreciate that. It makes this whole thing much easier."

"I can't say I imagined Homeland Security taking an interest in our little operation here," Parker said as he sat at the head of the table. "But I think you'll find it quite impressive. I hope you don't find me too obnoxious with my immodesty, especially since we haven't gotten all that much to show off yet. But I've got a good team with me. We're just tracking an impressive, and ever illusive, prey."

Sydney was immediately on alert. The guy was as pleasant as Weiss had said he had been when they met. Sydney didn't entirely trust pleasant people in her line of duty. Maybe she was just being a little overly sensitive. Or maybe she had been burned too often in the past. Either way, the easygoing manner and the willingness to work together triggered Sydney's defenses.

Luckily, Agent Hughes looked suspicious enough for the both of them. She kept staring at each member of the APO team like she was trying to read their minds. Sydney found it rather unnerving, to say the least.

"So what is it that brought David Lowell to your attention?" Parker asked, getting right down to business.

None of the APO agents was willing to answer that question, not even to provide the preset cover story. It wasn't that they didn't have something to tell Parker. They had a lie all ready and prepared for the man. They just weren't willing to use it yet. It was finally Dixon who raised the concern Sydney knew all three of them shared. "Before we get into details," he said, "we were wondering—"

"About security?" Parker guessed. "Sorry, I

should have walked you through that first thing. Caryn?"

The woman sat up with perfect posture and addressed the group in what could pleasantly be described as a condescending tone. "Every morning we run a sweep of the office to check for listening devices. Every room has a sound inhibiter that will block any external equipment from hearing inside. Additionally, the walls of *this* room are lead lined—and the glass is several inches thick, so that when that door is shut, a bomb could effectively go off in here and no one would know."

"Cheery thought," Weiss said.

Hughes shot him a death glare. "In case you thought you were dealing with amateurs here, let me assure you, we know what we're doing."

"We never suspected otherwise," Sydney said. "We just need to make sure this information doesn't get out."

"It goes no farther than this room," Parker assured them. "Caryn is my number-one operative. No one else in the organization needs to know unless we agree that they can be told. Okay?"

"Okay," Weiss said as he leaned in to the table. "You've been watching Lowell for what? Three years?"

"Two years and change," Parker replied.

"And in that time he's transported millions of dollars worth of drugs across the border into America," Weiss said.

"A few million less than he would have had we not been watching," Hughes said tersely. "We may not have stopped him, but we've definitely slowed him down considerably."

Weiss's eyes popped and he looked horrified by his own faux pas. "I didn't mean it as an indictment against your work," he assured them. "I just meant he's done a good job at getting things past customs."

Sydney was pleased to see Weiss was going with the "blame a third party" tack. Suggesting Lowell's continued success was the fault of customs agents would go a long way toward ensuring that the DEA officers didn't feel like they were under attack. But Sydney did feel that things needed to move along a bit, so she chimed in. "We think he's planning to start moving more than just drugs across the border."

Parker nodded his head in agreement. "I've always thought that was a possibility. Lowell's not the kind of man that's ever happy with what he's got going on. He's always looking for the next big score." He leaned back in his chair. "So what are we talking about?"

"Chemicals," Weiss said, "the kinds that could be used in biological terror."

A laugh immediately burst from Hughes. "That's ridiculous. Lowell's not a terrorist."

"We never said he was," Dixon quickly added. "But that doesn't mean he's not interested in *selling* to terrorists. He certainly doesn't mind who he sells his drugs to."

Sydney was hoping Parker and Hughes would buy the story. Going from drugs to chemical weapons wasn't that far of a stretch. It was certainly more believable than the truth. No telling what Hughes's reaction would have been if they had said that Lowell was actually developing mind-control drugs. She probably would have laughed them out of the building. It was a nice benefit that their cover story was more plausible than the reality.

"I don't know," Parker said. At first Sydney thought he was just as skeptical as his coworker, but he was addressing his reaction to Hughes. "We have heard about him being in contact with some shadier players than normal, foreign leaders and such. I never believed it was just because of his work with world hunger organizations. Mind you, nothing's been substantiated yet. But we knew he was up to something."

"But terrorism?" Hughes asked. "Parker, that's so far out of his league—"

"And when has David Lowell ever been satisfied with his current level of power?" Parker asked. "The man is more obsessed with growing his business opportunities than Donald Trump."

"We're under the impression that he's got a stockpile of chemicals," Weiss said, continuing his story, "maybe in some kind of lab where he's developing the weapons. That part's unclear."

"What kind of lab?" Parker asked, as if he was on to something.

"That's the question," Sydney said. "It's probably not a large space. The lab itself is probably just a room. They'd need some storage, obviously, but nothing major. It would probably be out of the way, so it wouldn't attract too much attention."

"And they wouldn't want too many people around, for safety reasons," Weiss added.

"But someplace they could blend in at the same time," Dixon said.

"Basically, they could be anywhere," Weiss concluded. "Which is why we need to get into Lowell's compound, hack into his computer, and see if we can find a location for this laboratory where he's developing and storing these chemicals."

"Well, I'm not sure that's entirely true," Parker said with a glance toward Hughes. The look was clear to Sydney. He knew something. And now it was even clearer that he was going to milk the moment for all it was worth. This was his chance to show the Homeland Security contingent that his team hadn't been sitting around on their duffs for a couple of years doing nothing.

"I'm guessing you have some useful information for us," Weiss said, playing along. "Don't keep us in suspense, man, spill it."

"Well," Parker said with a grin, "we'll do everything we can to help you get into Lowell's compound and to his computer, because you're going to need to do that to get the access code. There's just no two ways around that. We know. We've tried. But as for the part about *finding* the lab? I think we might already know where it is."

CHAPTER 10

"The lab is in a warehouse in Toronto's industrial district, just off the four-oh-four," Weiss said as his way of opening the video conference call. What better way to impress Arvin Sloane than by having the information they had been sent to determine before they had even made their first scheduled report?

"We got the address from the DEA," Weiss continued, addressing the monitor on his laptop. Sydney and Dixon had joined him in his hotel room for the meeting. They were all seated around the small dining table. Onscreen was an image of the APO conference room in Los Angeles, where the rest of the team was gathered around a camera and looking back at them through the wall of monitors.

"I suspected as much," Sloane replied. "Lowell does have a lot of holdings in the city. It was likely the DEA would have checked them out."

Weiss was temporarily dumbfounded. It was all he could do to keep his jaw from dropping and stumbling over his own tongue when he spoke. Arvin Sloane was never quick with praise. To him a job well done was simply a job that was done. But was it too much to at least *acknowledge* that it was impressive that they accomplished their primary objective on the first day? He could see that Nadia, Marshall, and Vaughn all looked impressed. Even Jack had a grudging smile on his face, and that man never smiled. But Sloane looked like he was waiting for them to move on to the next issue.

Granted, all Weiss had done was ask the DEA agents for the information, but he had laid the groundwork for cooperation between the two groups. They had certainly found the location of the lab faster than they would have if they had gone with Sloane's plan of bringing Felicia in.

Weiss quickly recovered enough to move the meeting forward. "The problem is we need access codes to get into the building," he explained. "The DEA has made several attempts to get inside, but all have failed."

"Yes, but does the DEA have a Marshall Flinkman?" Marshall asked rhetorically. "Did I just refer to myself in the third person? Yes. I guess I did. I *hate* when people refer to themselves in the third person. It's so pretentious. Please forget—"

"Do you have anything that could get us inside, Marshall?" Jack interrupted, bringing the meeting back on track.

"Well, first I'd need an ID on the locking system," Marshall said. "I do have a few pieces that should be able to get through any door."

"But we don't know about any security redundancy," Weiss said. "Once we get past the main door, there could be additional security. Without Lowell's files, there's no way to tell until we get inside, so it will be impossible to plan for every contingency."

"Impossible?" Marshall asked with giddy smugness. "Or a *challenge*? Think about it."

"We still think the best way to get inside is

through Lowell," Sydney added gently. "Besides, we've got to get the FBI files back and whatever else we can get on Lowell to bring him in. We can't just leave him walking around freely knowing all about Sway and how to make more of it. The only way to do that is by going with the original plan and getting access to Lowell's compound, which Dixon and I already have, and while we're at the compound we'll somehow get the codes to the lab."

"Or we could always just drop a couple of bombs on the lab and the compound and be done with it," Weiss joked.

"I think the Canadian government could very well take that as an act of war," Sloane replied with deadly seriousness.

"Yes . . . I mean . . . that wasn't an actual . . ." Weiss mentally kicked himself for forgetting that Sloane didn't have much of a sense of humor. His eyes, naturally, went to Nadia on the screen. Just seeing her face was both reassuring and an added stress. As comforted as she made him feel, he didn't want to look like an idiot in front of her. *Or any* more *of an idiot,* he ruefully thought.

"We've made arrangements to work with the DEA simultaneously on both matters," Sydney jumped in. "While Dixon and I are at Lowell's compound in Thunder Bay, we'd like Vaughn and Nadia to work with DEA Agents McCormack and Dodd on getting into the lab. Once we retrieve the information from Lowell, Weiss will forward the access codes along with any other security information they would need. From that point, it would be their mission. Going in at night, the four of them should be able to take the lab with minimal force."

"I don't like the idea of the DEA agents having access to the files and the drug," Sloane said. "If that information gets out . . ." He let the statement hang in the air for a moment.

"We're covered on that end as well," Dixon said. "We've made it clear to Agent Parker—he's the lead DEA agent—that while we are willing to share resources, we are going to be the lead agency on securing the lab and all related materials. Once the lab is secured, the DEA agents will maintain the perimeter while Vaughn and Nadia wipe the files and destroy the evidence—all in the interest of national security, of course."

"And the DEA finds that plan acceptable?" Jack asked.

"They don't love it, but they'll play along," Weiss

said, glad that things were back on track. "This Parker guy seems on the up and up. I trust him."

"Fine," Sloane said. "Vaughn and Nadia will be there in the morning." Sloane turned from the camera to address the two agents in the room with him. "Once you've secured the lab, please obtain some samples of Sway before destroying the rest of the stockpile. The FBI lab would like to use it to continue their research. In the end, this could actually prove useful to their efforts. They hadn't gotten nearly as far as Lowell has."

"But . . . we can't," Nadia said.

Even over the monitor, Weiss could see that Sloane was visibly taken aback by Nadia's refusal. "And why is that?" he asked his daughter.

"Because it's against the law," Nadia said, "and numerous treaties the United States has with foreign governments—*my* government, for one. Didn't the FBI learn from their mistake when they lost the files in the first place? Sway is too dangerous. It should all be destroyed."

"That's not the new mission," Sloane said. "Our orders are to retrieve samples of the drug as well."

"But it's wrong," Nadia said.

"That is not our decision to make," Sloane said.

"Why not?" Nadia asked. "What's wrong with telling Chase we refuse to do it? This drug is too dangerous to be left in anyone's hands. Doesn't part of our job to protect the country include protecting the country from itself?"

Sloane ignored his daughter. He was done defending the instructions he had already given. "Agent Weiss, this is an order from Director Chase. Please see to it that the team follows through on the assignment."

Weiss looked at the screen, willing himself to focus on Sloane and him alone. He could feel Nadia's eyes on him even across the two thousand miles that separated them. Weiss had agreed with everything Nadia was saying. He had been under the impression they were just going to recover the missing files and destroy everything else. He was well aware of the fact that Nadia wasn't the only one who shared this opinion. Most of his team did not like the idea of Sway existing, even if it was going to be under the control of the U.S. government.

As team leader, it was Weiss's place to register the formal complaint for his people, but the look in Sloane's eyes told him that a challenge would be a lost cause. This was a direct order that needed to be followed. A discussion was not going to be an option at this time. If only he could have explained to Nadia what was going on in his head. But, considering he couldn't even bring himself to look at her at the moment, there was no way he could possibly use silent communication to get the idea across to her.

When he realized everyone was waiting for him to speak, Weiss said the only thing that he could, given the situation. "Yes, sir."

The ensuing tension ran so deeply that it seemed even Marshall could sense it back at APO headquarters. "Um . . . Sydney? Dixon?" he said tentatively. "Since you're going to need to access Lowell's computer to get the codes for his lab, I've got something I can send up with Vaughn. Actually, I've got several things I can give him, but I'll narrow it down to the most useful and just send that."

"Thanks, Marshall," Weiss said, both for the technology and for moving the conversation along. It only took a few more minutes of conversation for them to wrap up business. Weiss considered asking Nadia to stay on the video conference for a moment, but figured that wouldn't look very professional. He could always give her a call later to discuss his inability to come to her defense. Not that the inaction was all that defendable in his own mind.

Once they terminated the connection, Dixon went to his room to give his children a call. Weiss assumed that Dixon was really just making an excuse to leave because he knew that Sydney would need to stick around to do some mop-up duty.

"Don't let him get to you," Sydney said as soon as the door was shut behind Dixon. "That's just the way Sloane operates. You're doing fine."

"It's not that," Weiss said. "It's Nadia. I think she expected me to jump to her defense and insist that we destroy all samples of Sway."

"That's not your decision to make," Sydney said. "And you would have been fighting a battle you had already lost. Sloane wasn't going to change the order. Nadia knows that."

"But I still should have spoken up," Weiss insisted. "If he weren't Nadia's father in addition to being my boss, I would have said something. I don't think Sway should be out there, no matter who controls it."

"If there's one thing I know, it's about uphill battles with Sloane. It's not over yet. There's still time to make the argument when we get back," Sydney said. "It will be easier once we have Sway in hand. Then we can all express how we feel about what to do with it. Until we have the drug, it's a fairly useless discussion. Sloane would prefer we focus on the mission and put aside any of those pesky moral issues. That's just the way he is."

"Still, it would be easier if he and Nadia weren't related," Weiss said.

"It would be easier if our little group wasn't so damned incestuous," Sydney said. "I didn't mean that in the literal sense."

Weiss chuckled. "I know what you meant. But you can't help falling for someone when you spend so much time with her in tense situations. Did we learn nothing from the cinematic masterpiece that was *Speed*?"

"There's that devil-may-care attitude we've all come to love," Sydney said. "Look, don't worry about Sloane. You're not going to win with him—ever. And right now it's not even important. It's not like he was around when Nadia was growing up. They didn't even know about each other. Nadia's still working through her feelings about him. His opinion isn't worth all the weight you're giving it."

Weiss knew that Sydney was trying to be helpful, but she was missing the point. "That's true at the moment," he said. "But at some point his feelings about me are going to come into play. And aside from all that, he's still my boss and I need to have some kind of professional relationship with him. I need his respect."

"True," Sydney said. "But he doesn't need to agree with you to respect you."

"Well played," Weiss said as they shared a smile. Now that he'd finally put some of his own issues to bed, he noticed that Sydney seemed a little distracted. It was almost like she wanted to say something, but wasn't sure how to ask. She kept looking at him, then subtly turning away. "What?"

"Nothing," Sydney said as she rose from her chair and tried to move for the door. "I should get some rest. Big day tomorrow."

He gently took her by the arm. "Hey, you dealt with my problems, it's only fair that I stick my nose into yours. Isn't that what friendship's all about? Now stick around. We can have a sleepover, talk about how cute we think Vaughn is, and do each other's hair. It'll be fun."

Through the laughter, Sydney looked both uncomfortable and relieved at the same time. "Okay," she said as she sat back down. "Vaughn is pretty cute, isn't he?"

"You never heard that from me," Weiss said. "Now, what's the problem?"

"It's not a problem," Sydney said. "Not really, anyway. It's about Vaughn's mom."

"A lovely lady, indeed," Weiss said.

"Is she?" Sydney asked. "I mean, I assumed that, but . . ."

"You still haven't met her, have you?"

"Well . . ."

"It's just that things have been crazy," Weiss said, quickly coming to Vaughn's defense and saving Sydney from having to place any blame in the first place. "What with Lauren and everything else."

"Exactly!" Sydney said, relieved.

"But that doesn't mean you don't want to meet her," Weiss guessed.

Sydney nodded.

"And you don't know how to bring it up to Vaughn," Weiss concluded.

"It's just, after everything he's been going

through with his dad lately . . ." Sydney trailed off, not sure how to continue.

Weiss wanted to prompt her to go on, but managed to hold it back. He knew that Vaughn had been having some issues with his father's death, and possible resurrection, lately. Vaughn had told him as much, although the guy never really went into too much detail about what was going on. But this wasn't the time for gossip, even if it would ultimately help his friend.

"And you don't want to put a strain on his relationship with his mom?" Weiss guessed again.

"I thought this might not be the best time," Sydney said.

"But she's going to love you," Weiss said without a doubt in his mind. "You're perfect for him. Heck, you're better for him than he deserves. His mom will see that."

"That's what I'm hoping."

"Then again," he said, "she did like Lauren. So the woman's not exactly the best judge of character."

"You're a big help," Sydney said, but she was laughing, so it seemed like he had done his job to relieve at least some of her concerns.

Since he finally elicited a smile from her, Weiss

decided it was time to turn serious for a moment. "It's not like Vaughn's trying to keep you from meeting her, if that's what—"

"I didn't—"

"I know," he said. "But it's not like he's thinking about that at the moment. What with you two and your whole 'we're taking it slow' business, he probably just hasn't realized. Bring it up. He'll be fine. You really should meet her. She makes a mean cobbler."

Sydney laughed. "Peach or apple?"

"I don't know," he said. "I was making that up. But every mother should know how to make a mean cobbler."

"Thanks," Sydney said as she got up again to leave the room.

"No, no," he said. "Thank you."

Weiss showed her to the door, taking care to lock it behind her. Not that he expected anyone to try to sneak in during the night, but it didn't hurt to take a few extra precautions. He did have enemies in this town, whether they knew they were his enemies yet or not.

Weiss looked over to his laptop, knowing he'd have to go over the mission plans at least once before bed. He also needed to make a call to Nadia to make sure everything was still okay between them. Both of those things could wait a moment. First he needed to collapse onto the bed and take a moment for himself. Running the mission was already hard enough. But dealing with Arvin Sloane in the process was turning out to be much more stressful than he had anticipated.

CHAPTER 11

LOS ANGELES

Arvin Sloane felt uneasy, but he couldn't pinpoint exactly why that was. He would have said he was nervous, but that was an emotion with which he was not intimately familiar. Fear he knew. He had long since conquered fear, except in deeply personal matters. But this gnawing concern wasn't something that he usually allowed himself to experience. Though the world dealt deeply with shades of gray, for Sloane everything was very much in the realm of black or white. He preferred the extremes. He had no time to be bothered with uncertainties like simple nervousness.

A tap on the doorframe roused him from his unsettling emotions. He looked up to see his daughter, Nadia, standing in the doorway. Just once he wished that she would look happy to see him. Even when they weren't having a disagreement, there never seemed to be that look of contentment that Sydney invariably had on her face when her father was around—that is, if they weren't in the middle of one of their routine estrangements.

"Confused" was the best word to describe the way Nadia seemed when she was with Sloane. He couldn't blame her, really. She had gone her entire life without knowing anything about him. Then, finding out his entire history at once—the whole biased reporting of it—had probably come as a shock, not to mention the brief time they had spent together in Siena had understandably affected her growing relationship with him. But still, it would be nice to see her come to him with a different look on her face once in a while.

"I have the mission workup as requested," Nadia said brusquely as she handed him a file. "I don't think it will be a problem keeping the DEA agents involved but uninformed of the true nature of the mission. As long as they don't start asking the lab workers they capture questions, there shouldn't be any reason for them to think they've found anything other than chemical weapons."

"If they are well-trained agents, they won't deviate from the plan," Sloane said. He didn't like relying on unknown elements like other agencies, but he knew there was no choice in the matter. One of the problems with operating with a black ops mission statement was the inability to clearly coordinate with other agencies. Granted, not having to coordinate with other agencies was also the benefit of black ops, but there was always a trade-off between the two.

"Speaking of deviating from the plan," Nadia said as she slid into the seat across from Sloane. It was an odd move. Most of his agents didn't sit unless they were invited to do so. Knowing what was coming, Sloane was tempted to dismiss her as if she were any other member of his staff. But, as his daughter, he knew that turning her away without hearing her out could affect their personal relationship. These were the kinds of adjustments that he had to get used to now that his newly found daughter was under his employ.

That said, he didn't have to kowtow to her completely, and tried to cut her off before she could even broach the subject. "You know my thoughts on the matter. It is a direct order and it needs to be followed."

Sloane turned to his computer to finish the e-mail he had been working on when he was distracted by his own nervousness. Sadly, that feeling had only increased since Nadia had entered the room. His final statement, and the fact that he had gone back to work, should have told his daughter that their conversation had ended. Unfortunately that did not turn out to be the case.

"But can't you go back to Director Chase?" Nadia persisted, refusing to leave her chair. "Suggest that Sway is too dangerous to be trusted to anyone. The government shouldn't have been doing the tests in the first place."

"The government does a lot of things it shouldn't be doing," Sloane reasoned. "Many of those things ultimately turn out to be for the greater good."

"How could this mind-control drug possibly be for the greater good?" Nadia asked. "It's already fallen into the wrong hands."

"An unfortunate accident."

"Accident?" Nadia scoffed. "Sway didn't happen accidentally. David Lowell knew exactly what he was doing. The FBI lab was on track to create the same thing, just without the catchy name. What is the FBI going to do with it when it gets the drug back? Start using it on prisoners? Force people to work against their own governments? Brainwashing through a tiny pill?"

"That, Nadia, is not our concern," Sloane said. "The government has ways of policing itself."

"But—"

"I have listened to your concerns," Sloane said politely but forcefully, "twice. They are noted. However, I have been given an order and that order must be followed."

"I mean no disrespect," Nadia said, causing Sloane to brace himself for the coming disrespect, "but how many times in your career did you go against an order and do something for your own benefit? Wouldn't this be for your benefit as well? Aren't we all served better by a government that finds ways to protect us without breaking treaties and relying on science that messes with our minds?"

Sloane couldn't help but think that Nadia's motivation had something to do with what he had put her through earlier in the year. Using Rambaldi's elixir to force her into recalling the muscle memory that created a map to the prophet's endgame had been a miscalculation. No matter the result, he was still haunted by the images of Nadia under the control of that liquid, forced onto her in dangerous amounts by Sark and Lauren. But, even though he understood her motivation, he could not justify her beliefs.

"Noble sentiments," Sloane said, "but flawed logic. You are already assuming the worst-case scenario. We don't know what the government lab intends to use this drug for. We don't even know what the original files pertained to. Sway could have been nothing more than David Lowell's bastardization of humanitarian research."

"You don't seriously believe that?"

"I believe nothing," Sloane said, "other than the fact that we have a mission to tend to and orders to carry out."

"I don't think—"

"You've made your opinion perfectly clear," Sloane said with a forced note of finality. "And I have allowed you to debate it further than I normally would allow one of my agents. If you want to lodge a formal complaint, you will need to take it up with the mission commander."

"Weiss is in Canada," Nadia said. "By the time we get a formal complaint in, the mission will be over."

"But the drugs will still be in our possession for a while before we turn them over to Director Chase," Sloane reminded her, kindly but firmly. "Just because we complete the mission as ordered does not mean we can't keep the discussion open. But at this point, it is only your opinion. Agent Weiss is in command of this mission. If he feels that it warrants further discussion, then we can proceed. Otherwise, we are done here."

Nadia finally took the message. Sloane tried to ignore the hurt look on her face as she slowly got up from her chair. He turned his attention back to his e-mail as she left the office, passing Jack Bristow on the way out.

"What are you doing?" Jack asked from the doorway.

Sloane wanted to ignore the man. He could almost anticipate the conversation that was about to ensue. "I'm *trying* to compose an e-mail," Sloane said with more than a note of annoyance. "However, others are attempting to keep me from my work."

"I meant," Jack said as he also took a seat without asking permission, "what are you doing with Nadia?"

Sloane refused to take his eyes off the computer screen. "I know what you meant, Jack. I don't see how it's any of your business."

"You're right, Arvin, it's not," Jack said. "But in some inescapable way I am tied to you and, in part, to Nadia. And I cannot sit back and watch you destroy your relationship before it's even begun. Inevitably, that will come around to affect Sydney. And that I will not allow."

"So, what is it you're concerned about now?" Sloane asked, finally turning to face Jack. Sloane knew full well just how adamant Jack could be about personal loyalties. Better to let him have his say and move on than escalate the issue into a confrontation somewhere down the line.

"Did Chase really insist on us retrieving samples of Sway or was that your idea?"

"Jack, I'm surprised at you," Sloane said.

"Your accusations are usually much more circumspect."

"Aren't we both getting a bit too old for these games?" Jack asked.

"Isn't it up to our children to keep us young?" Sloane made what he thought passed for a joke. "That is what I've heard. Of course, I am new to parenting."

"Don't do this," Jack implored.

"Again, what is it you think I'm doing?"

"You're playing games with Eric Weiss," Jack said simply.

"I assure you, Jack, that is the last thing that is going on here," Sloane said. "Agent Weiss is not at issue."

"Why did you put him in charge of this mission?"

"It was his idea," Sloane said. "Odd how I'm being accused of mistreating my employees by giving them responsibilities entirely in line with their job descriptions."

"You know what I mean."

"Do I, Jack?" Sloane asked. "And, more importantly, do you know what *I* mean? I have been charged with commanding an organization staffed with people who dislike me, for whatever reason. This is complicated by the fact that I am trying to build a relationship with a daughter I was never given the chance to know. And now some stunted man-child is interested in that daughter. Why would you possibly think I have any objection to him?"

"You can't win this way," Jack warned. "I know. I've tried it myself."

"I realize that, Jack," Sloane said. "But this isn't some childish game I'm playing. I am running an organization charged with keeping the country safe from terrorism. Eric Weiss is an active member of that organization. The fact that he seems to be dating my daughter has no place in my assignments. This is his mission. The success or failure of it is entirely dependent on him and him alone."

The two men stared each other down for a moment. Jack looked like he had more to say on the subject, but they were interrupted when Marshall came bursting into the room. Never before had Sloane been so happy to be interrupted by the man, though he was concerned by the nearly apoplectic mannerisms Marshall was exhibiting.

"Um . . . excuse me, sir? Uh . . . sirs?"

Marshall said. "I think we have a problem."

"What is it, Marshall?" Sloane asked as he pulled his gaze away from Jack.

"Those DEA guys up in Canada, they've been doing some digging into those aliases we created for Sydney, Dixon, and Weiss," Marshall said as he nervously shifted from one foot to the other.

"Fine," Sloane said calmly. "That is why we created them in the first place. I don't see the problem."

"Well, it's not just that they're looking into the aliases, so much as they're looking really *closely* at them," Marshall said. "*Really* closely. I mean they're digging things up, down, and all around trying to get background information that simply isn't there. I've got my staff working to block the inquiries at every turn, but as soon as we fill one hole in the information flow, the DEA guys come at it from another angle. It's like they're doing everything in their power to prove our team isn't who they say they are, which they aren't, so eventually the DEA is going to find something. Or, more accurately, *not* find something, which is tantamount to finding something, in this case. Do you follow?"

"No, Marshall," Sloane said. "I do not follow."

"Well, I was saying—"

Sloane held up a hand to halt any additional rambling. "No, Marshall. I understand what you are saying. I just do not see any reason to panic. If the DEA team finds a few holes in the aliases, it will not be the end of the world. They will just assume it is classified information, or something similar. At any rate, their superiors in Washington have been briefed on the nature of those aliases and will stand by what they have already been told. There is nothing to worry about."

"Really?" Marshall said, with a mixture of relief and continued doubt. "Because if I was doing the background research—"

"Thank you, Marshall."

"Oh, okay," Marshall said as he turned and left the room. If only it had been that easy for Sloane to dismiss Nadia—or Jack, for that matter.

As soon as Marshall was gone, Jack addressed Sloane. "You're not concerned about the deep background checks in the least?"

"Not at all," Sloane said. "The DEA team will do as ordered. This mission will not be in effect long enough for them to find anything truly damning. As I see it, we're perfectly fine."

"Are you going to warn Weiss at least?"

"I see no reason to," Sloane said. "Why complicate matters? It seems to me he is already nervous enough for some reason. I do not wish to risk putting the mission in jeopardy over a trivial concern."

Jack shook his head. "It's nice to see how you're handling things, Arvin. It makes me feel so much more comfortable with the mistakes I made with Sydney."

CHAPTER 12

THUNDER BAY

"Nice place you got here," Weiss said as he, Sydney, and Dixon dropped their bags in the DEA Thunder Bay office. To actually call it an office was a bit of a stretch. As far as Weiss was concerned, they were in what a travel brochure would lovingly refer to as a cozy hunting lodge with all the modern amenities. It was the kind of place one would take the family for a weekend getaway, not to set up a stakeout to keep tabs on an international drug lord.

The cabin was a short ride out of Thunder Bay

and worlds away from the bland office setting in Toronto. But the key to any good stakeout was blending in, and out in the middle of nowhere, it wasn't like the DEA was going to find a plethora of commercial real estate. The cabin was only a half mile from the edge of Lowell's property, so it was perfect for its convenience alone. Considering how far out they were, a half mile was almost the closest thing to being neighbors.

On the ride out Parker had explained that the DEA had been renting the place since the operation began over two years earlier. To date, they still hadn't managed to net anything from the expenditure. Lowell's compound was impossible to breach, even with the most advanced listening devices.

"We tend to use it more for its intended use," Parker said ruefully. "Makes for a nice getaway, but a lousy listening post."

It was a comfy setup, Weiss noted. They were standing in one large multipurpose room that began as a living room but continued into a kitchen/dining room, and culminated in an office space. A single door led off to what Weiss assumed were the bedrooms and bath. The great room was done up in dark shades of brown and had all the creature comforts by way of rustic furniture. There was a noticeable lack of a television, but an expected amount of computers and electronic surveillance equipment in the office space. Weiss couldn't help but notice that the equipment looked like it was collecting dust.

Weiss checked his watch. They were right on time, which was a relief considering they had been dealing with delays all afternoon. Because of the intense drizzle that had continued for three days in a row in Los Angeles, flights out of LAX were backed up, making it difficult for Vaughn and Nadia to get into Toronto in a timely manner. Of course, Caryn Hughes was loving every minute of delay and treating them as if it was an indication that Weiss—or Sammy, as they knew him—didn't have a clue what he was doing.

Vaughn and Nadia had finally arrived minutes before Weiss's team was scheduled to leave for Thunder Bay. There was barely enough time to say hi, much less introduce them to Dobbs and McCormack, with whom they were going to be working on taking out Lowell's lab. Weiss had wanted to pull Nadia aside to talk about what had happened the night before during the video conference, but there wasn't time. He barely managed to sputter out an apology for not calling her after the meeting. If only he hadn't kept pushing back the call to go over the mission op. Falling asleep in one of the hotel chairs while at the computer hadn't helped either. It hadn't been good for his relationship or his back.

It was clear that Nadia was still upset over the order to return with samples of Sway. But Weiss still wasn't sure if she was angry with him for his silence, her father for his insistence on following orders, or the both of them for those reasons and more. Now he had to put that aside and focus on the plan. He couldn't allow for any more distractions. There was too much at stake.

"Okay," Weiss said as he opened up the case that Marshall had sent along with Vaughn and Nadia. "Considering how Lowell is about security, the less you bring, the better. I'm thinking this is all you're going to need." He took out a cigarette case.

"This is a nonsmoking stakeout," Hughes said with her usual lack of charm.

Weiss did his best not to roll his eyes and sink to her level. "According to our tech guy, it should be able to break though most computer security programs and download the contents of the hard drive. That should provide us with everything we need to bring Lowell in and get the lab access code."

Parker held out a hand. "May I?"

Seeing how proprietary Marshall was with his technology, Weiss considered refusing to hand the item over for Parker to look at. However, that wouldn't exactly foster familial relations between the two teams, so Weiss let him take a look and made a mental note to forget to tell Marshall about it later. "Here."

Parker examined the equipment thoroughly. Weiss could tell by the expression on the guy's face that he was impressed. "Nice," Parker said as he handed the device back to Weiss. "Homeland Security, right?"

"Yeah," Weiss said, a little more quickly than he had intended.

"You guys have access to some impressive stuff," Parker said. The way he was slowly nodding his head suggested that he didn't quite believe that they were who they said they were. Or maybe, Weiss thought, he was just being overly sensitive.

He ignored the feeling and set up his laptop on the kitchen table. "Once we get the access code for the lab, we'll send it to the B team," Weiss said as the computer booted up. "You know, as opposed to the A team. But I pity the foo . . ." He trailed off when he saw Hughes shooting daggers at him with her stare. "I'll have communications up in a moment."

Parker and Hughes worked to open up the place while Sydney and Dixon got a look at their surroundings. Weiss would have preferred to fill the silence with some idle chitchat, but it was already clear that Caryn Hughes didn't like him, simply because he was in charge of the team that had wormed their way into *her* investigation. He wasn't about to give her any genuine fuel for her anger.

Weiss understood how she felt. He'd been steamrolled before when he was at the CIA. In fact, it seemed like that had been former Agent Stephen Haladki's mission in life back when they started working with Sydney on the SD-6 project. But that was different. Haladki was a jackass with delusions of grandeur and immediate advancement. Weiss was just doing his job here. And he would have sworn he was doing it with his usual charm and panache.

That usually won over the most difficult audience.

"Communications are up," Weiss announced as he punched in the final command on the computer. An image from the small camera sewn into Vaughn's black ski mask came onscreen. He was looking at the exterior of a dark and dreary warehouse. So far, there wasn't much of anything going on.

"Shotgun, this is Houdini," Weiss said into the microphone attached to the laptop.

"Houdini?" Hughes snorted.

Weiss continued, ignoring her. "Can you read me?"

"I've got you, Houdini," Vaughn replied.

Weiss had briefly considered altering their call signs for this mission. Considering they were working with the DEA agents under false names, it would have made a certain amount of sense to change their call signs as well. But that was a level of nit-picking that Weiss wasn't ready to achieve quite yet. It was one thing to be careful, it was quite another to be totally paranoid.

"And here's a little shout out to Merlin," Weiss added softly, making sure Parker and Hughes weren't listening first. "I know you're out there in radio land, and it's much appreciated." Weiss paused to wait for a response, even though he knew he wasn't going to get one. Marshall was online to observe the mission in case anyone back at headquarters was needed for any reason. Since the mission profile didn't really call for interaction with APO, it was simply an added precaution Weiss had thought up. Marshall had been instructed to keep radio silence. He was probably in his office playing video games while he kept the mission on as background noise.

"Patching in the rest of the team," Weiss said at regular volume as he typed in commands to activate the communication systems on Nadia, Dobbs, and McCormack. "Shotgun, please confirm status."

As soon as the official report began, the others joined Weiss around the computer screen. They could see part of Dobbs's face through the camera while they listened to Vaughn's voice. "I've taken position on the north side of the building with D-one," Vaughn reported. "Evergreen is covering the south with D-two."

"D-one and D-two?" Hughes asked. "Don't we get fun little nicknames like your guys?"

"Okay, Caryn," Parker said. "We got it. You're annoyed. Move on."

Weiss was glad to see he wasn't the only one

taking issue with her attitude. He couldn't help but think that Arvin Sloane would never be disrespected in this manner. All it would take from Sloane was one of his patented death stares to stop Hughes cold. Then again, Sloane's death stares often came with the backing of actual death behind them. It wasn't a trade-off Weiss was willing to make.

"How's it look?" Weiss asked. The image onscreen now showed little more than a wall with a door beside an empty lot.

"Most of the staff cleared out at five," Vaughn reported. "We've seen some people coming out for smoke breaks, but no new staff has entered the building. I'm guessing the night shift is a skeleton crew. Shouldn't be too much of a problem."

"Good to hear," Weiss said over the comm. He contemplated giving some kind of positive reinforcement over communications—possibly something that Nadia would interpret as a message for her, since she was also listening in. Of course, the DEA agents with the team were also listening, as was everyone in the room. Instead Weiss had to settle for a simple "Keep on alert. We'll contact you when we have the information."

"Shotgun out," Vaughn replied.

Everything seemed set on that end. All Vaughn needed was the access code and any other security protocols and they'd be free to infiltrate the lab. Weiss was glad to hear that most of the staff had cleared out of the building. It would make things much easier when the team went in later. A full security detail was probably still in effect, but at least with the regular lab rats gone there would be fewer people to get in the way or take up arms against the team. All they needed was the signal and Weiss's first leading role on an APO mission would be a success.

He immediately gave himself a mental kick for jinxing his mission with blind optimism. Yet, at the same time, he couldn't help but have hope. *I love it when a plan comes together,* he thought.

"So it looks like it's on us now," Sydney said as she took the cigarette case and slipped it into the pocket of her blazer. She had chosen a form-fitting pantsuit for the evening's festivities. It was an attractive outfit, with the added benefit of allowing her a free range of movement should things get physical—though hopefully they would not.

Dixon had also opted for stylish yet casual

attire. It looked as if the two of them were heading for a dinner party. Of course, they both knew not to accept anything to eat or drink from Lowell—or especially Felicia—considering they had witnessed firsthand how dangerous that could be.

"Don't screw it up," Hughes said lightly, though there was a serious undercurrent to her words.

"That's enough, Caryn," Parker said. She clearly did not like to be put in her place, but she also knew better than to say anything else.

Sydney and Dixon said their good-byes and went out to the car.

"It's the wait that always kills me," Weiss said as he watched his team pull out onto the road.

"We can only hope," Hughes said. Weiss thought that, under different circumstances, he could be friends with the woman. They certainly shared a biting sense of humor. Assuming she was actually joking.

"Look," Weiss said. "We don't need to work together much longer. What say we try to be civil and get through the night and then we can all go our separate ways?"

"Easy for you to say when you breeze in here holding all the cards," Hughes said.

"Caryn," Parker said with a warning tone.

Weiss held up a hand. "That's okay. I can take it. But now that you mention cards, anyone carrying? I figure we can get in a few rounds of Texas Hold'em. It's all the Hollywood set is playing nowadays."

Hughes looked at him more coldly than she had since they met. "I need a beer."

Weiss raised an eyebrow but didn't say anything. He had already caused enough problems simply with his mere presence. He wasn't going to give her any more reason to hate him by questioning her practice of drinking while on duty.

Still, she picked up on the concern. "Yes, Mr. Homeland Security," Hughes said as she walked to the refrigerator. "We're allowed to have a beer—one beer—while on stakeout. Sometimes it's the best way to get over the fact that there's nothing else to do."

"Hey, I'm always up for a little postmission celebrating," Weiss said. "Save one for me."

Hughes opened the refrigerator and spent way more time looking in it than should have been necessary, in Weiss's opinion. "Damn," she said. "Empty."

"Well, considering you know we don't keep this

place stocked with beer, that shouldn't really be a surprise," Parker said as he pulled a deck of cards out of the desk.

"I don't need *you* being a wiseass now," Hughes said.

"Why? You think you have the market cornered on that?" Parker said as he sat at the kitchen table and started shuffling the cards.

"I'm going out," Caryn said as she threw her jacket on and went for the door. "Beer run."

"Could you pick me up some Tic Tacs while you're out?" Weiss asked. He should have expected the slammed door that came in response. As the room stopped shaking, Weiss turned his attention to Parker.

"She's a bit territorial," Parker explained.

"A bit?"

Parker motioned to the seat across from him for Weiss to sit as he absentmindedly continued to shuffle the cards. "We've been on this case for a couple of years now. No leads. If you guys come in and put it all together in two days, it's going to look really bad for us, no matter who winds up taking the credit officially. Caryn's been through this kind of thing before. It's why she's on my team and not leading it."

"Well, I understand that," Weiss said. "But it isn't exactly my fault. I'm just following orders."

"She knows that," Parker admitted as he stopped shuffling. "She just doesn't care. Course, it would be a lot easier if we really believed you were who you say you are."

Weiss froze. "Excuse me?"

Parker smiled warmly. "Just because we haven't been able to get the proof we need to take down Lowell doesn't mean my guys can't do their jobs. Take background research, for instance. Dobbs and McCormack are pretty good at that."

"Really?" Weiss asked. "And what have they found out about me? I do admit to a few unpaid parking tickets, you know. But that's public information last I checked." Weiss figured he could disarm anyone with his humor, and he was prepared to go to the well to deal with this latest twist.

"Well now, they haven't found all that much out about you or your friends," Parker said. "Which is saying something right there, don't you think? There's a surprising lack of information about you guys beyond the files from Homeland Security."

"You came to determine that in less than one day?" Weiss said. He trusted that Marshall had been blocking any queries about their aliases over the past twenty-four hours. There couldn't be too much information to find. "Doesn't seem fair to develop your opinion on us so quickly. Barely had a chance to get to know us."

"I'm not making any judgments," Parker said. "Yet. Just wanted to let you know we're looking, is all."

"Well, I'd expect nothing less," Weiss said.

"Now, about that card game? I hope you brought some money to lose."

Weiss leaned back in his chair as Parker dealt the cards. Oddly enough, he felt like they had just played their first hand.

Weiss felt utterly useless at the moment. There was nothing to do until Sydney and Dixon came back, hopefully with the information. A few rounds of cards wouldn't hurt in the meantime. Weiss had no intention of betting, though. His mind was distracted enough as it was. Parker's latest announcement didn't help much either. If Weiss was going to play with money, he could have just handed it over to Parker directly to save time.

CHAPTER 13

"We have an appointment with Mr. Lowell," Sydney said into the intercom at the front gate of Lowell's compound.

"Names?" a voice shot back at them.

Sydney provided the set of aliases they had given to Lowell the previous day. She was careful not to use the names that they had told Parker and his people.

She guessed the names alone had been the magic words, because the gates swung open in front of them without another query from the disembodied voice emitting from the intercom.

"I guess we're expected," Dixon said as Sydney pulled forward.

Sydney drove down the winding road that led to Lowell's compound. It wasn't a typical driveway, as the house still seemed to be a ways off. Surveillance photos from a satellite in orbit hadn't been very helpful in giving them the lay of the land. Sydney wasn't even sure how far she had to drive, since the road twisted around the trees. The design choice probably had a lot to do with keeping the house totally invisible from the main road.

Along the way she saw a pleasant little sign warning guests to remain on the path. She suspected this had to do with the intensive security they'd all heard so much—and so little—about. As she drove she tried to pick up on the telltale signs around her to indicate what defenses were in place. She was hoping that they'd be able to get out of the house without rousing any suspicion and simply drive back the way they had come. That was what she considered the "perfect world" plan. But Sydney had learned long ago that she did not live in a perfect world. Far from it. Therefore, it would be best to know what she'd be dealing with if she had to leave the compound through a more expedited route.

Aside from some well-placed video cameras, she didn't recognize anything beyond the basic perimeter guard they passed after they had entered through the gate. No dogs. No strategically placed weapons. Nothing. Of course, she knew the best security was invisible.

"Looks pretty clear," Dixon said, echoing her silent concern.

"That's what I'm worried about," Sydney said as she continued up the road.

After another minute the path opened up, giving her the first view of the house. Tall trees lined the circular drive, running almost right up to the walls of the building, which helped keep the full size of the house a mystery. Aside from the beautiful canopy of leaves the trees created, Sydney knew they served a purpose of obstructing any satellite photos taken from above. Having seen those photos earlier, Sydney had to admit the trees did their job well.

In keeping with the surroundings, Lowell's home looked very much like a mountain lodge, constructed of wood that probably came from the local lumberyards. The house had a definite Frank Lloyd Wright feel to it, but it was far too modern to have been designed by the late architect. Sydney assumed that Lowell had designed the place himself. The man was actually an architect in his other life. That wasn't just a cover story. In his early forties, David Lowell was too young to have been a student of Wright's. Even so, it was clear to Sydney that he had certainly designed his home in homage to the man.

Between the trees she could see that three stories of the building were offset against one another in a step design that carried up the foot of the mountain that it had been built next to. With Lake Superior along the southern edge of the property and a hill leading up to a sheer cliff above, it would be especially difficult to sneak up on the house from two of the four directions. The fifth direction—up—was even more of a challenge. Even from the ground, Sydney could see through the treetops that the route from above would be almost impossible for even the most experienced climber. Once again, she couldn't make out any noticeable security on the cliffs above, but the descent itself would probably kill most people.

"Hate to see what this place is like in the rainy season," Sydney said, wondering if any storms brought down a shower of boulders from time to time. The house looked pretty formidable, but the placement of it against the foot of a rocky cliff definitely broke with the rule of "form follows function"—unless the function was to protect from intruders, which Sydney had to admit the property was designed to do very well.

Lowell and Felicia were waiting at the front door for Sydney and Dixon as they got out of the car. The way the criminal pair was locked arm in arm confirmed that Weiss's research had been correct. They were more than just employer and employee.

Walking up the long wooden staircase to the first level of the house, Sydney thought the four of them looked just like two friendly couples getting together for a weekend retreat. If it weren't for the obvious two-member security detail stationed on opposite sides of the driveway, she would have felt like she should have brought a bottle of wine.

"Welcome to Shangri-la," Lowell said as he received his guests and they exchanged their greetings. "I know the name isn't that original, but the rest of the place makes up for that, in my not-so-humble opinion."

Sydney braced herself for even more overly polite banter as they played their games. If anything, he was already being more pretentious than he had been at the garden party only a day earlier. "A lovely home you have here," she said, taking in the spectacle of a house and looking for additional security features. "Did you design it yourself?"

Lowell's face lit up with excitement over what Sydney thought would have been an obvious question. "Why, yes I did. Would you like to take a look around?"

"We would like that very much," Dixon said. Sydney didn't need to catch his eye to communicate what they both already knew. The offer had been extremely fortunate. A tour of the house would be incredibly helpful to Sydney for when she had to sneak out later, find Lowell's computer, and download his files. She didn't expect that he was going to take her through any secured areas, but getting a lay of the land would be helpful enough. At the same time, she wondered why a man who was known to be so security conscious would be willing to give a tour of his highly secured compound to virtual strangers.

The tour began in the library to the left of the foyer. There Lowell showed off the new humanitarian award he had received the previous day at the garden party in Scarborough. He used the opportunity to scold Sydney and Dixon yet again for not staying around for the ceremony and forced them to sit through a word-for-word reenactment of his acceptance speech. Sydney plied him with false apologies, not caring if they were enough to sate the man's stunning ego.

He went on for a good fifteen minutes as he continued to show off the many other awards and accolades he had received over his years of service to the community. Sydney wasn't sure what the point of the act was, but listened politely. Why he thought his guests would be interested in hearing about him rather than getting down to business was unusual. But Sydney had done business with more than her fair share of unusual people in the many years she had been involved with undercover work.

"But we're being rude," Felicia said out of nowhere as she headed for the bar. "We haven't offered our guests any drinks."

Sydney and Dixon shared an unnecessary look

between them. This was all part of the act. "No, thank you," Dixon said. "We think we'll pass."

"Are you sure?" Lowell asked.

"Positive," Sydney replied. "Alcohol goes right to my head. You know how that is, right?"

All four of them smiled politely when Sydney finally mentioned the elephant in the room. She didn't add that irons also went to her head when Felicia was around. Instead she just hoped that the implied reference to Malcolm Norwood would steer the conversation toward the subject of the evening, but was soon disappointed by the response.

"On to the living room," Lowell said as he led the tour across the hall. In this room he highlighted the built-in features of the shelving and other such instances of design genius. He was rightfully proud of the house he designed and the many facets that he had taken into consideration in the design stage that would only serve to enhance the finished product. Truly it was a beautiful place that would have been featured in architectural magazines, if it weren't for the illegal operations the owner ran from somewhere inside its walls. Splashy photos for all the world to see wouldn't exactly be the best way to keep law enforcement from getting a good idea of the layout of his compound. Too bad this was the one area of his life where his ego was squelched by his security concerns.

As Lowell went on about his fabulous built-ins, Sydney heard someone—presumably security—come in through the front door and walk through the foyer. She checked her watch to note the time in case the guards took regularly scheduled rounds, making sure to keep her ears open for the guard passing by later. At the same time, she tried to get a good angle to see if it was one of the men from outside. Unfortunately Lowell had them in the opposite corner of the room. There was no way to see out to the foyer without going across the room to do so. And there really wasn't a way to do that without drawing their attention along with her.

Sydney wondered just how much of the house they were going to see before they got down to business. As she had already seen from the outside, the place was pretty large. Even though she didn't have an exact measure of the actual size, she estimated that a tour moving at this speed would work their way through the entirety of the house by midnight at the earliest. There was suddenly no doubt in her mind that Lowell was stalling for some reason.

Thankfully Dixon picked up on that as well. "Really, this is a wonderful home that you have," Dixon said as they left the living room, "but we were hoping to discuss your . . . it *is* safe to speak in here, I assume?"

"Perfectly," Lowell assured them. "You see that blinking red light up there?" He pointed to a corner of the ceiling where a small panel was nestled into the wall. "There's one in every room and in every hall. Each one blocks any kind of electrical transmissions from getting in or out of the building."

"Must be difficult on your cell phones," Sydney said.

"And on any wireless system we try to set up," Lowell conceded.

"We rely on actual wires to keep us connected here," Felicia explained. "The system I've set up is one-hundred-percent secure. And each of those panels also scans its respective room intermittently throughout the day and night to make sure no one has bugged the place for recordings they can come back and pick up later. All approved electrical devices are run through the main system. Anything not on that line will register with security.

"Good thing I didn't wear my digital watch," Dixon said as they moved to the stairs.

"Yes, it is," Lowell replied seriously as he took them up to the second floor.

Sydney was glad to see that they were bypassing the dining room and kitchen. Hopefully they'd be able to wrap things up soon and move on to the real reason for coming to the house. All the while she was taking detailed mental notes for when she could sneak away later. At the very least she now knew where the internal video cameras were placed and was already plotting ways around them so security wouldn't catch on to her moves later.

"The banister is an especially interesting piece," Lowell said as they continued the tour. "I had it brought over from an English manor that used to belong to the royals. It was a kind of secret vacation home, away from the press."

"This is all very interesting," Dixon said abruptly, "but we did come here with a purpose. I am interested to hear more about Sway."

Lowell nodded as he pointed out the artwork on the second floor. "Certainly. I just thought you'd like to see the place. We can talk as we walk."

"And we'll certainly continue to appreciate the

design of the house as we go," Sydney said, soothing his ego.

"Naturally," Lowell said.

"Why don't we go up to the office?" Felicia suggested. "It's a much better place for us to conduct business."

"Yes," Lowell said excitedly. "And I can show you the view of Lake Superior. It is really *spectacular.* For that very reason I designed the entire house just so that room could be built above the tree line."

"Must be hard to get any work done," Dixon commented.

"I manage," Lowell said as he led them to another stairwell.

Sydney couldn't help but think Dixon's comment and the response were as much about the view as they were about the fact that Lowell's business dealings seemed to be the last thing on his mind. That wasn't exactly logical considering the man was so eager to make a name for himself in his new endeavors, not to mention the fact that he had gotten quite far in both his legal and illegal businesses. If it took him this long to make a deal every day, it was amazing that he wasn't homeless.

"So, about this Sway," Sydney said. "How did you come up with such a wonderfully insidious little drug?"

"You know what they say," he replied. "Ninety percent inspiration. Ten percent larceny—with the help of our friend, Mr. Norwood, of course."

"May he rest in peace," Felicia added with a sickening grin.

"And how much stock are we talking about?" Dixon asked.

"How much are you interested in?' Lowell asked. "We're almost past the testing phase. We want to make sure we know if there are any nasty side effects. Honestly, I didn't think it was ready for the market, but Norwood jumped the gun on us." Lowell started laughing for no particular reason. "No pun intended."

Sydney did not find what passed for humor with these people to be the least bit funny. "Obviously we've already seen the product tested," she said, "but what are the parameters of the drug? How long do the effects last? Is there a counteragent?"

"I wouldn't want to buy a stockpile that is immediately useless because a simple antidote becomes readily available."

"All in due time, my friends," Lowell said as he reached a cherry wood door. "All in due time. But first, I'd like to show you the heart of my empire, right behind this door."

Sydney couldn't believe they were going to be so lucky as to be brought right to the computer from which she needed to pull the information. With Dixon in the room to act as a distraction, it would be child's play to pull down the files. The cigarette case device Marshall had developed just needed to be placed within a foot of the hard drive. She didn't even need to attach it to anything; if she just took it out and asked if it was okay to smoke inside the house, the job would be done. The hard part would be finding a way to activate it without setting off the alarms.

As Lowell slowly twisted the doorknob, Sydney realized that this had suddenly gotten too easy. There was no way a man with Lowell's rumored preoccupation with security would just usher them right into his base of operations. Sydney tensed, preparing herself for what could be on the other side of the door. As always Dixon was right there with her, and she watched as his hand curled into a fist.

"And here it is," Lowell said as he pushed the door open. "The hub."

Sydney braced herself as she looked into the empty room. No one was there waiting for them. No secret army was prepared to attack. It was just as Lowell had said: a simple home office. Of course, it was four times the size of any home office Sydney had ever seen, but it was just an office nonetheless.

A pair of his and hers matching desks with computers, phone banks, and assorted office materials sat on one side of the room in front of a row of file cabinets. On the opposite wall a door stood ajar. From what Sydney could tell, it seemed to lead to a bathroom, though she couldn't fully see inside.

The other half of the room had what looked to be a conversation area with a couch and some chairs. Beyond that was the huge picture window, displaying what Sydney had to admit was a pretty spectacular view, even in the darkness of night. She could see boats lit up in the distance out on Lake Superior moving slowly across the water.

But that was all that was waiting for them in the room, nothing more.

Sydney relaxed slightly as she turned her attention to the computers while Lowell led her and

Dixon into the room. The feeling of relief, however, was short-lived. As soon as Felicia shut the door behind them—and locked it—she pulled a gun out of her blazer and rudely aimed it at her guests.

CHAPTER 14

"Please have a seat," Lowell said as Felicia pointed them to the conversation area. Sydney was concerned about the kind of conversation that would require a gun, but did as instructed. She knew that the best thing to do at the moment was hear their hosts out. There was no need to act rashly until she and Dixon knew what was going on. In the meantime, they would try to talk their way out of whatever problem they may be having.

"If this is the way you conduct business, it's no wonder Mr. Norwood turned on you," Dixon said.

"For every minute you keep that gun aimed at us, I'm knocking another million dollars—*U.S.* dollars—off my original offer."

"Over there." Felicia ignored him as she waved the gun toward the two high-backed chairs that faced away from the window.

Felicia handed the gun to Lowell and she pulled two sets of handcuffs out of the desk nearest to the door. She walked over to Sydney and Dixon and chained each of their wrists to their respective armrests. That done, she retrieved her gun from Lowell and took up a position beside him. Sydney had to give the woman points for keeping a gun on them even though they were effectively immobile at the moment. She was obviously a student of the school of "better to be safe than sorry."

"This is outrageous," Dixon said as he pulled on his restraints.

"You can drop the act, Mr. Secret Agent Man," Lowell said with a considerably less pleasant tone than he had been using earlier. "I'm onto your plan to get your hands on Sway and try to take me in. I mean, did you really think you could come here and just walk away with everything you wanted in two days? I have been dealing with people like you far too long to be done in so easily."

Sydney ignored the egomaniacal ranting and focused on the task at hand. There was obviously a way out of this predicament. All she had to do was find it. In the meantime, she didn't have to play into Lowell's game. "I'm guessing it would be pointless to tell you we don't know what the hell you're talking about."

Felicia let out a burst of laughter. "Yes, it would."

"So, what, you have some grainy video or some overheard conversation that leads you to think we're with . . . what? The DEA?" Sydney asked, testing the waters.

"Not at all," Lowell said. "We know you're with Homeland Security. We know your names are Sylvia Newton and Chris Soto. And we further know that there's something more going on here that we haven't entirely figured out. But, all that aside, may I say that I am honored to have caught your attention so quickly. True, it will make my life a little more difficult, obviously, but having the United States government raise my profile will ultimately help my business endeavors in the long run, I think."

The ego on this man never quits, Sydney thought.

She focused her attention on the chair she was bound to. The wood on the armrests seemed thick, but certainly not unbreakable. She had gotten out of similar situations before, using the chair itself as a weapon. It didn't seem so heavy that it would impede her movement. If only she could find the right distraction, she could make her move. The gun and being tied to a chair were obstacles, but not insurmountable ones.

Sydney hardly heard what Lowell was rambling on about. It was all white noise to her. She was too busy silently communicating with Dixon. Years of partnership had honed their skills of wordless speech. Lowell and Felicia knowing they were Homeland Security meant one of two things: Either Lowell *did* have the DEA offices bugged, or he had a mole in the organization. Considering the DEA agents were the only people who thought she and Dixon were with Homeland Security, the news had to have come from them one way or another.

When Sydney realized that Lowell had finally stopped speaking, she figured it was time to go on the offensive. She hadn't given up on the idea of talking their way out of this. "So you've learned our secret identities," Sydney said, going with a diluted version of honesty. "Congratulations. It doesn't really change our reason for being here."

"I assume you're here to arrest me," Lowell said. "That would probably be easier if Felicia didn't have a gun on you at the moment."

"Obviously there's been some misinformation bandied about," Dixon said. "We're not here to arrest you. We couldn't care less about your drug smuggling. You've gotten us confused with the DEA agents who have set up camp in your life. We're only interested in retrieving those stolen files and taking control of your entire stock of Sway. Being that those are our only concerns, we have been instructed to make an offer—a *generous* offer, as we mentioned earlier—to that end. We're here to do business with you, not take you into custody."

"And we have a considerable budget at our disposal," Sydney added to sweeten the deal.

"So the U.S. government is now willing to bargain with what it perceives as criminals?" Lowell asked skeptically.

"You know what they say about desperate times and measures," Sydney said, playing along. The government would never come up with the kind of money Lowell would be asking. That's why they relied on black ops units like APO to go in and do the dirty work. And even if they did have the budget to buy him off, Sydney would have still wanted to see him behind bars for a good long time. Or, better yet, in an insane asylum. *What kind of person takes you on a tour of his home before holding you hostage?*

"Do you actually think I would take you up on your offer?" Lowell asked as he came around and sat on the couch facing them. He still wasn't close enough for Sydney to make a move, but she took his willingness to move toward them as a good sign. Felicia remained behind Lowell, standing over his right shoulder, holding the gun on them.

"Aside from the fact that I hardly believe you," Lowell continued, "has anything I've said led you to believe I'm in this for the money? I know you didn't get the full tour, but I think it's pretty obvious that I'm doing quite well on my own. This is about positioning. Putting Sway on the market and leaking the fact that it was research developed by your government that led to the creation of the drug . . . well, I think the fact that I stole that research and put it to use will get the attention of the right people."

"Congratulations," Sydney said. "You're a star." She no longer worried about antagonizing him. She had finally found a weakness to exploit. The coffee table in front of her was built in a star pattern, with one of the points in front of her. It looked like it was made from a fairly formidable, though thin, wood. All it would take is a well-placed kick and she could send the table up at Lowell and Felicia. The distraction would be enough of an opening for her and Dixon to attack. She just needed to wait for the right opportunity and find a way to let Dixon know what she was doing. Luckily Lowell's penchant for rambling discourse was as good a distraction as anything she could come up with.

"I *am* a star," he insisted. "And you will be too. I think the loss of two—what I imagine to be *high profile*—agents from a United States government organization will add to my quickly rising stock. Of course I'll have to step down from my day job at Lowell and Associates. Don't want to taint the business with my new reputation. But that was always just a means to an end."

"Is this the part where you tell us all about your evil plan and how you're going to kill us?" Sydney asked. "Because we'd really appreciate it if you could wrap things up here. We're on a schedule."

"He's stalling because he knows the ending will be anticlimactic," Dixon said. "He's just going to try to force Sway down our throats and tell us to kill each other."

"Well, if that's the case," Sydney said as her eyes went from Dixon to the table, then up to Lowell, "I'd like to see him try."

When Sydney turned back to Dixon, their eyes locked for a moment. "So would I," he said, indicating that he was on to her plan.

"Oh, he's not going to force it down your throats," Felicia said. Just then, Sydney felt a pinch in her shoulder. When she turned to see what had happened, she saw Caryn Hughes standing beside her with an empty needle in her hand.

"You see," Felicia continued as Hughes looked on, "we've been able to distill Sway into liquid form."

Sydney felt the cold sliver of liquid Sway race through her arm and into her body. She had been caught off guard by Hughes and now it was too late to make a move as she found yet another gun aimed at her and Dixon. She silently cursed at herself for letting her guard down again. Hughes had obviously been hiding in the bathroom, waiting for her moment. She must have been the person that came in the front door while they were in the living room. Sydney worried what that meant for Weiss and Parker back at the lodge, though she didn't want to think about the possibilities.

"Are you okay, Syd?" Dixon asked.

"Yes," she replied with uncertainty. She felt fine at the moment. Her mind had not clouded over. She felt no particular need to do as she was told. Malcolm Norwood had reacted to the drug quite quickly, but he had ingested it. There was no telling what the reaction time was when it was injected into the bloodstream. Somehow Sydney didn't think it would be any slower than if the pill had been crushed up in a drink. If anything, the direct route it was taking through her body to her brain was probably even faster.

As Sydney contemplated her options, Hughes moved behind Dixon and swiftly wrapped a gag around his mouth. Sydney was surprised by the woman's quick, almost frantic movements, but it made total sense in hindsight. If Dixon had just warned Sydney not to listen to anything she was told, the Sway would be rendered useless. She had learned that much from the boy in the club who had intended to take a swan dive from the balcony. Once she had warned him against jumping, it was like his command had changed. He had done exactly what she had told him. Sway was obviously an equal-opportunity mind-control drug, meaning anyone who gave an order would have to be obeyed. With Dixon gagged and nothing but enemies in the room, she had to move quickly, before the drug took effect.

"Sit still," Lowell said, like he was talking to a rambunctious child.

At first, the command made no sense to her. Sydney wasn't moving in her seat. She was already sitting still. But when she did try to move, she found that the effect of his words was immediate. Sydney could not move. She *wanted* to move. She even tried to force her body to shift in the seat. But it was to no avail. It was almost as if she had been injected with a paralyzing agent. She was effectively trapped in the chair.

"Amazing, isn't it?" he asked. "I'm told you feel quite normal right now, is that right?"

Sydney didn't respond.

"I asked you a question," Lowell said. "Please answer me."

"I feel fine," Sydney replied against her will. It was the strangest sensation, feeling the words form in her brain and having them forced out of her mouth. She had been given truth serums before, but they usually had a drugging effect that almost made her feel removed from herself so she wasn't aware of what was going on. This was different. She had her full faculties available to her, yet couldn't do anything with them.

"Perfect," Lowell said as he got up and walked over to her. Hughes pressed her gun against Dixon's head, warning him not to move as well. Meanwhile Lowell lowered his face to within inches of Sydney's. She wanted to spit at him, but couldn't even bring herself to do that. "I've witnessed this numerous times with our test subjects," he said, "but this is the first time I've used it on someone truly against her will. I'm intrigued to know if the drug will be strong enough to overcome your resolve."

"And if it can't, isn't it nice to know you've got two people ready to shoot me if I do manage to move?" Sydney said. "Big man."

Lowell straightened up. "Lower your weapons," he commanded. The two women did as they were instructed, though they both looked hesitant to do so. Dixon may have been tied up, but he was still in control of his body.

"Talk about having no will," Sydney said, glad to see that at least her attitude had managed to break through the drug. "Did he slip a little Sway into your drinks, girls? Go ahead, Lowell, tell them to jump now. I want to see how high they can go."

"Shut up!" Hughes said.

Sydney's mouth immediately clamped shut. She still had enough free will to play off it though. With the new command, she guessed she was released from the "sit still" order, because she was able to shrug her shoulders and adopt an innocent look on her face as if she had simply decided she had nothing more to say. She could see that Felicia was amused by that at least.

Nice to know I can still be entertaining even without my rapier wit, Sydney thought as her mind continued to search for other ways to get out of this.

"Just for my own edification," Lowell said, "was it true that the U.S. government would offer me a big payday to turn over Sway?"

Several responses popped into Sydney's head, but she was unable to say any of them. If she wasn't so frustrated, she probably would have laughed.

It took a moment for Lowell to realize the problem. "You may speak."

"You have got to be out of your mind," she finally said.

"So, that's a no," Lowell guessed correctly. "A shame. I might have considered the deal, if the price was right."

Sydney wished he would just get on with it. She was getting tired of him talking just to hear the sound of his own voice.

"Moving right along," Lowell said as he circled the chairs, "Caryn has filled me in on what's going on here. And in Toronto. Of course, by now you've realized that with Caryn on our side, that warehouse in the big city is not what you were led to believe it was. There's no lab there. There's no Sway waiting for your little band of heroes." Sydney had come to suspect as much when she first saw Caryn, but knew there was nothing she could do about it at the moment.

"Caryn's been a wonderful help to us over the years," Lowell said. "Always kept us abreast of the DEA plans. Quite a little impediment to that wonder boy Agent Parker and his plan to take down the big bad drug lord. By the way, I have to admit I like that title. 'Drug Lord.' So much better than CEO in my opinion."

"Can you just tell me to kill myself and get this over with?" Sydney asked. Dixon said something through the gag. Sydney couldn't make it out, but she assumed that it was something along the lines of "Me too."

"All in good time," Lowell replied. "But first, I need you to kill a couple other people." Lowell turned to his security chief. "Felicia?"

The woman finally holstered her gun and went for what Sydney assumed to be Lowell's desk. She took a piece of paper from the desktop and walked over to Sydney, holding it in front of her face.

"Memorize this number," Lowell commanded.

Sydney looked at the seven-digit number. "Done," she said.

"You're sure you got it down?"

"It was *seven* digits," she replied, annoyed that he would think that was some kind of difficult task.

"Good," he said. "That is the code to get into my 'lab' in Toronto. You will fulfill your mission and provide that number to your superior officer. I assume you realize by now that I have a nice surprise waiting at the lab for your team."

Sydney's eyes narrowed to slits. Though she was glad to hear that Weiss was still alive, she didn't like this turn of events. Sure, she had figured that Lowell was going to try to use her to kill Dixon. She had never imagined that he would use her to put Vaughn and Nadia in danger as well.

"After the code is transmitted," Lowell continued, "I want you to take out the two agents back at the DEA surveillance station: Agent Parker and your superior officer, *Sammy*, is it? Then you can allow Caryn to kill you. Of course, I'd like you to put up a small fight so she can claim it was self-defense and continue to work on the inside for me."

"Hey," Caryn said. She seemed bothered by the fact that Lowell was giving Sydney permission to beat the crap out of her. *Can't imagine why,* Sydney thought.

"I said a small fight," Lowell reasoned with his underling. "Don't worry. You're going to get the final punch." He turned his attention back to Sydney. "Any questions?"

"Do you really think you're going to get away with this?" Sydney asked, largely to stall for time.

"For some reason, I think I already have," he said cockily. "Oh, and one more thing. From this point forward, you are only to take orders from Felicia, Caryn, or myself. No one else. And you cannot do or say anything that will tip off your fellow agents to the fact that you are not under your own control. Do you understand?"

"I understand," she said.

"Good," he said. "Caryn will show you to your car. Once you're outside, give her a few minutes lead time, then institute my plan."

Felicia tossed a set of keys to Caryn, who used them to unlock the handcuffs and free Sydney from the chair. "This way," Caryn said as she moved to the door, passing the keys back to Felicia as she went to leave.

Involuntarily Sydney rose from the chair and started to cross the room. Using whatever force of will she had left, she paused and turned back to Dixon. She knew the concern in his eyes was entirely for her and not for himself.

"Oh," Lowell said, "don't worry about your friend here. He'll be fine for the time being. And don't let on that he's in trouble either. I have a few calls to make and Felicia's got an errand to run.

But later we'll try out another sample of Sway to see what other kinds of government secrets he can spill for us. Then, of course, he'll be joining you on the other side."

Sydney tried to close herself off from having to hear his ridiculous attempt at what would have reasonably been considered "maniacal laughter."

"Go ahead," he prompted her. "Get moving. Time, as they say, is money."

Sydney exchanged one last look with Dixon before she felt her body turning back toward the door.

CHAPTER 15

"Gin," Weiss said as he laid his cards down on the table.

Parker stared at him for a moment. "We're playing poker."

"Oh," Weiss replied without looking at the cards. "In that case, full house." He tried to laugh, but his mind was elsewhere. The fact that the cards he had just laid on the table were no consistent suit of anything was the last thing on his mind. Usually on a mission he was in contact with the rest of the team. But it wasn't like he could sit around and chat with Vaughn on stakeout. Well, he probably could, but it wouldn't be prudent with all the DEA agents listening in. The bigger issue was that it was physically impossible to know what was going on with Sydney and Dixon while they were on Lowell's property. The man's impressive communications jamming equipment saw to that.

This was the hardest part about leading the mission. It had been Weiss's idea. His call. He was the one who had put Dixon and Sydney in the middle of this. And yet he was also the one who got to stay behind. It didn't seem fair. Granted, this was what Sydney and Dixon did every day on the job. There was nothing new here, except he was now the one entirely responsible for them.

Then there was Nadia. It was bad enough that he was concerned for Sydney and Dixon's well-being, but his thoughts of Nadia were an added source of frustration on top of it all. The last thing he wanted to do was fail in front of her. It would effectively show Sloane that he, Weiss, didn't know what he was doing. And that would add to the already strained relationship between father and daughter. Weiss knew that was the last thing he should be worrying about on a mission where actual lives were at stake, but he couldn't help it.

"Your mind's not really in the game here," Parker said.

"Sorry," Weiss replied. "I guess I'm not really up for cards. I can show you some magic tricks if you want." He figured all kids liked magic tricks and Agent Parker wasn't much more than a kid himself.

"I didn't mean the *card* game," Parker replied as he gathered the deck. "I meant the mission. You're distracted. And I can tell it's more than just worrying about your people. Trust me, I get it."

"I don't mean to be rude, but you don't know what's going on in my head right now," Weiss said as he pushed back his chair. He needed to be up. He needed to be moving. "I don't even know what's going on in my head right now."

"You're afraid of this mission failing," Parker said as he watched Weiss pace the room. "And it's killing you that your people are out there and there's nothing you can do about it. Hey, I've been on this assignment for a while now. I know how you feel."

"That's different."

"How?"

"You're a *kid*," Weiss said. "What are you, twelve? I've been doing this kind of thing for a bit longer than 'a while.' I was running missions while you were fumbling around in the backseat of your dad's car trying to get to third base with your prom date."

"So, what's the deal now?" Parker asked.

Weiss considered telling the kid the truth. He'd probably never see Parker again, so it didn't matter if he shared any real personal information. It's not like the guy could use the situation to track Weiss back to APO. "It's my new boss," he finally said.

"Hardass?"

"The hardest," Weiss said. "And he just happens to be the father of my new girlfriend."

Parker looked at him with a new understanding and obviously decided it was time to change the subject instead of commenting on the situation. "Where *is* Caryn with that beer?"

"Right here," Hughes said as she came in the door.

Weiss didn't bother looking at her. She'd only hit him with more harsh words.

"And where's the beer?" Parker asked.

"They only had Canadian brews," she said as

she sat down on the couch. "After a couple of years out here, I've gotten a bit tired of the stuff. You know what I mean?"

"Not at all," Parker said.

"So, what'd I miss?" Hughes asked.

"A rousing game of cards," Parker replied. "I told you we should have invested in a TV when we set up this place."

"Can't stand television," Hughes said. "Rots the mind. Speaking of which, what's *his* problem?"

Weiss noticed that she was staring at him while he paced the room. He didn't bother to say anything. Her attitude was the least of his concerns right now.

"Leave it be, Hughes," Parker said. It was the first time that Weiss had heard him call her by her last name.

She didn't have time to retort. They were all distracted by the sound of a car pulling up to the house. Weiss and Parker exchanged concerned glances. "I didn't expect them back so soon," Parker said.

"Neither did I," Weiss said as he took out his gun and went to the window.

Weiss pulled back the curtain to get a look

outside. The rental car they had taken out at the airport was stopping in front of the house and Sydney was getting out. Dixon was nowhere to be seen.

"Where's . . . Chris?" he asked as soon as Sydney came in. It took him a second to remember Dixon's proper alias in front of the DEA agents.

"He stayed behind to make it look like he was completing the deal with Lowell," Sydney said. "But he wanted me to go on ahead and pass the access code along so they can take the lab."

"You left him behind?" Weiss asked. He knew that wasn't like Sydney at all, but she didn't seem concerned.

"He'll be fine," Sydney said.

"Not if we take the lab," Weiss said. "If the team goes in, someone could report back to Lowell. He's going to know that Chris had something to do with it."

"He'll be fine," Sydney repeated.

"Give me the access code," Hughes said as she rushed to the computer.

"Wait a second," Weiss said. Something felt wrong here. Then again, everything had felt wrong since Sloane had put him in charge.

Sydney stepped past him and started reciting the numbers she'd memorized. "Six, five, two—"

"I said, hold on!"

"Three, five, seven, one."

"Sy—*Sylvia*," Weiss insisted as he followed Sydney to the computer. "Why did you leave your man behind?"

"Hey there, squirt gun," Hughes said into the microphone. "Wake up. We've got the access code."

"Caryn," Parker said sternly. "You did not get permission to relay the code."

"*Permission*," she said. "Trent, we have been on this mission for over two years and have absolutely nothing to show for it. We finally got our ticket out of this dead-end assignment. We can't sit around and do nothing."

"Go ahead," Vaughn's voice said over the comm, obviously unaware of what was transpiring on the other end of the connection.

Parker covered the microphone with his hand. "We've got a man unaccounted for," Parker said. "We need to confirm his status first."

"She said he's fine," Hughes said.

"He is," Sydney repeated.

"See! Now we've got to move."

"It's not my call," Parker said as he turned to Weiss.

"Houdini, are you there?" Vaughn asked, adding to the stress of the situation.

"Are there any other security precautions they need to be aware of?" Weiss asked Sydney. "Anything beyond the code."

"No," Sydney said. "It's all clear once they get through the door."

Something felt off to Weiss. It was too easy. But Hughes was right. They couldn't just wait around. They had to act. After a brief mental deliberation, Weiss stepped up to the microphone and waved Parker away.

"I'm here, Shotgun," he said into the mike, "and we've got the code."

Nadia listened as Vaughn read back the code to Weiss in confirmation. Once that was done, their team received the formal go-ahead. She nodded to McCormack. It was time to move. She was glad to finally get out of her stakeout position. She had been locked away in a warehouse for hours, keeping track of the south side of the building with

McCormack. The guy wasn't one for small talk, or any kind of talk at all, it seemed. Several times she had tried to engage him in conversation only to be met with muffled grunts in return. It didn't exactly make for an enjoyable night.

She was still upset with her father and, to a lesser degree, Weiss. She didn't understand why they weren't supposed to just destroy the stolen files and the entire stock of Sway. It didn't seem to her like anyone would be better served with that drug in existence. Even if the secret FBI lab managed to get tighter reins on their security, it would still eventually get out. Either someone else would steal it, or another country would catch on to what the United States had been up to and start working on their own version of the drug.

Maybe it was because she had been raised in South America, but Nadia wasn't as willing to trust the United States government as her father was. Then again, she still didn't trust her father as much as she wished she did. But Nadia had to put all that aside right now. It was time for her to focus on the mission, whether or not she agreed with it.

Nadia and the DEA agent slipped out of the abandoned warehouse where they had set up shop.

They were careful to remain hidden in shadows as they made their way to the north entrance, where Vaughn and Dobbs were waiting. They had confirmed the placement of all the security cameras in the hours they had spent watching the building. The DEA already had extensive information on the outside of the building and the surrounding area, but it helped to pass the time for them to double up and confirm that everything was where it should have been. The DEA information was correct. They had no problems with the external security on the place. It was getting in that had been their problem before. But now they had the code.

Nadia could sense McCormack's relief that his mission was finally nearing conclusion, but there was something else, as well. She assumed it had something to do with the fact that the APO team—or Homeland Security team, as they were posing—came in and wrapped things up in a little over twenty-four hours. She wondered if that was why he had had so little to say while they had been on stakeout. She knew how she'd feel if someone took all of her hard work, ignored it, and came up with a better solution to an ongoing problem.

"All clear?" Vaughn asked as Nadia and McCormack reached him and Dobbs.

"All clear," she replied. They had not seen anyone on their walk to the north side of the building. It looked like everyone had packed it in and finished up with their smoke breaks for the night.

"Okay," Vaughn said. "We don't know what to expect inside, but this mission has two goals."

"And you're going to tell us these goals, right?" McCormack asked. It was the longest sentence he had constructed in Nadia's presence since they had met hours earlier.

Vaughn ignored the attitude and continued. "Containment and eradication. First we need to take the lab workers into custody. We don't need them continuing their work elsewhere. Best I can tell there are only a handful of the science types inside. The real problem is security. We'd like to take them in too, but they're the ones who will put up the fight. Do what you have to do, even if it means taking them out."

"And containment?" Dobbs asked.

"That's our job," Vaughn said. "Once we get everyone out, she's going to wipe the computers, while I set the place to explode to destroy the stock."

"Wait a minute," McCormack said. "You're going to blow up biological agents? Aren't you worried about releasing toxins into the air?"

"The explosion will burn off the toxins," Nadia said, hoping to put an end to any argument.

"How can you be sure?" McCormack insisted.

"Because we're sure," Vaughn said with a note of finality in his voice. "Now let's move in."

Nadia pulled the small keychain Marshall had provided for the mission out of her pocket and held it up for the others to see.

"Going for a ride?" McCormack asked.

Nadia ignored him. "When I press this button, we'll have two minutes of electrical interference to disrupt the surveillance cameras, maybe two and a half minutes. Apparently the device is a little temperamental, according to our tech guy. At any rate, that will give us more than enough time to get to the door and punch in the code."

"Okay," Vaughn said as he pulled down his ski mask. "We go on my mark."

CHAPTER 16

Sydney Bristow was familiar with torture. Physical torture. Emotional torture. She'd been through it all. And that wasn't even counting the hellish period of six months she'd spent under the control of torture specialist Oleg Madrczyk. Thankfully she had blocked out most of those painful memories, even though she had forced herself to relive them once out of necessity. But no torture was worse than what she was experiencing at the moment. Knowing that she was having a hand in the deaths of the people she cared about most in the world was killing her. And there was nothing she could do about it but watch.

Sydney kept her eyes locked on the screen of the laptop at the DEA safe house as Vaughn gave his marching orders to the team. They were about to go in. Sydney didn't know what was waiting for them inside, but she suspected it wasn't anything they were prepared to meet. Something more than just the random people they had seen during their stakeout had to be in the building. But the question was, what? Sydney couldn't even be bothered to worry about the actual location or implications of the lab that they had been sent in to destroy. At this moment, the idea of Sway getting out to a global market was nothing compared to the possibility of losing Vaughn.

She could barely see her sister though the darkened video. Since the camera was mounted in Vaughn's mask, she couldn't see him at all. Inside, she was screaming for them to know it was a trap, but she couldn't bring herself to form the actual words. Even if she could manage, she saw Hughes was watching over her. The turncoat had her hand resting near her holster. If Sydney tried to warn Weiss or Parker, they would all be dead before she could get the words out, leaving Vaughn and Nadia to die just the same. She was so worried about them that she didn't even fear for herself. The fact that Hughes was supposed to kill Sydney when she was done killing Weiss and Parker was the furthest thing from her frenzied mind.

As long as they were still alive, Sydney had hope. As long as she was alive, she could do something to stop this. In addition to torture, her mind had already been through some of the cruelest procedures known to man. Some of those she had even experienced voluntarily. There was no way some drug was going to take total control of her. She refused to let it.

So far she hadn't been able to figure out a way to fight against Sway. But suddenly her father's image flashed into her head. It was a total "what would Jack Bristow do?" moment, and it gave her the answer she was looking for. No one could bend with the breeze the way her father did. The man lived his life knowing that sometimes he had to get his hands dirty to get the job done. Sydney refused to embrace that philosophy for the most part, although she had done a bit of bending of her own from time to time. The trick was to know how to bend without breaking. And in this case, that meant finding a way to make her instructions bend for her without breaking them.

Sydney knew that she couldn't warn Weiss and Parker. She knew that she was supposed to kill them. But the question was, how? She could easily shoot them both and put an end to it quickly. That's what Lowell would have wanted. But that wasn't what he had told her to do. He had left the method of murder entirely up to Sydney. The trick was finding a way to give them a fighting chance of survival.

Emphasis on the fighting chance, she thought as the answer fell into place.

Sydney would have to attack them and hope she could hold back enough not to overwhelm them from the start. The odds weren't in her victims' favor. Weiss was well trained, but he didn't have nearly the amount of experience with hand-to-hand combat that she had. Parker was an unknown, but considering he'd been on what amounted to a surveillance mission for over two years—combined with his young age—she suspected he wouldn't be that hard to take down. She was going to have to find a way to maintain control of herself during the fight and convince her body that there was no time limit on how long she could take to kill them.

She'd go after Parker first. Aside from the fact that it kept Weiss safer, that was the only way to ensure that she wasn't killed in the process. If she went for Weiss, there was a good chance Parker would intervene by instinct, taking her out without a second thought. But the other way, Weiss would hold back while he tried to figure out what was going on as long as Parker still had some fight left in him. Hopefully Weiss would jump to the right conclusion in time.

The screen on the laptop suddenly cut to static and they lost their audio feed. Nadia must have activated Marshall's jamming device to disable the surveillance cameras outside the warehouse. Sydney tried not to think about the fact that the cameras probably didn't even work in the first place. *Why set up cameras to protect nothing?* she thought to herself. The added downside of the electronics jammer was that the device cut off their communication as well. At that very moment they were walking into Lowell's trap and even if Sydney could try to find her voice, there was no way to relay the message to Vaughn and Nadia.

That's when Sydney had her second realization.

Lowell had told her to wait a couple of minutes before attacking Weiss and Parker so the Toronto team had time to get into the building. According to Nadia, they would be out of communication for at least two minutes, which meant they had effectively reached her time limit as soon as the screen turned to static since technically Sydney couldn't get back in touch with them for a couple of minutes. The static provided the delay that Lowell had requested. It was a loophole, but Sydney planned to use it to her advantage. It was time for her attack.

Weiss's heart jumped when the screen went to static. He had been looking at Nadia's face in the darkness one moment, and then it was gone. Considering he had a bit of his great-great-uncle Harry Houdini's skepticism in him, Weiss wasn't a big believer in signs. However, he did feel a figurative chill down his spine when seeing something that seemed like an ominous portent. Not that he hadn't expected the screen to cut to static when Nadia activated the electronics-jamming device, but it was unnerving nonetheless.

Not as unnerving, however, as when Sydney

suddenly let out a scream and jumped Parker from behind.

"What the hell are you doing?" Weiss yelled.

The answer was purely visual. Sydney had spun the DEA agent around and was beating him to a pulp. Parker was doing his best to defend himself, but his strength was no match for Sydney's blows. After the initial shock had passed, Weiss tried to pull Sydney off Parker by grabbing her right arm. She pulled back, taking his arm and flinging him over the couch. His head hit the coffee table, leaving him slightly dazed. When he got up, he noticed that Hughes was standing by the door, watching, but doing little else.

"Knock it off," Weiss said as he rushed Sydney. This time he managed to throw her off Parker. The man was bloodied and bruised, but still standing. Weiss didn't have the time to notice anything else. Sydney was on him in a flash.

Weiss blocked most of her blows, but he couldn't have landed a punch in return if he had tried. The inability to fight wasn't physical; it was mental. He couldn't bring himself to hurt her. It was quickly becoming clear to him that Sydney was under the influence of Sway. It was the only logical possibility.

"I said stop!" Weiss yelled as he managed to get both hands on her and pushed her back into the kitchen, slamming her into the refrigerator.

Sydney hesitated for a moment, but then pushed back, sending Weiss tumbling to the ground. As he lay there looking up at Sydney, she jumped over him, going for Parker once again. The DEA agent was reaching for his gun.

"No!" Weiss yelled. "She's under Lowell's control!"

Parker's eyes went wide. "What are you—"

Sydney never gave him the chance to finish the question. She kicked the gun from his hand and followed with a fist to the jaw that sent him reeling backward. Weiss knew that trying to intervene again was useless. Sydney was too good a fighter. But he had another idea.

"Hold on, Parker," Weiss called out as he went for the table. He grabbed the bag filled with Marshall's equipment and flung it open. There was a jumble of items inside. He cursed himself for not being better organized as he dug into the mess. Parker was barely managing to fight back and Hughes was still leaning against the doorframe as if she was enjoying the entertainment. It didn't require much deep thought to realize that she was working with Lowell. But Weiss would have to deal with that after he took care of Sydney.

He felt what he had been looking for at the bottom of the bag before he actually saw it. Weiss pulled out the small metal case Marshall had specially prepared for him. Inside the case were two rows of vials filled with a variety of liquids as well as a pair of injectors. Weiss quickly scanned down the rows and found the two vials he needed. He pulled the first one and loaded it into the injector, making sure to keep his back to Hughes the whole time. He knew it was risky to do that, but he couldn't let her see what he was doing.

Once the first injector was loaded, he jumped back into the fray. There wasn't time to do anything else yet. Parker was already down on his knees as Sydney continued to deliver blow after blow. Amazingly, the kid was still conscious, even under the assault. It was clear that Sydney had been instructed to kill. Weiss just hoped he could stop her before it was too late. He threw himself on top of Sydney and jammed the injector into her neck.

The effect was immediate. As Weiss got off

Sydney's back, she released Parker and backed away from him. "Thank you," she said as her knees went out from under her.

Weiss managed to catch Sydney before she hit the ground. Her body had gone entirely limp. She was out cold. He checked to confirm that her breathing and heartbeat were normal, then lifted her up and carried her to the couch. He didn't need to see Hughes to know that her gun was now trained on him.

"What the hell was that?" Parker asked groggily.

"Something I'm not allowed to explain," Weiss said. "But you could always ask her."

Parker finally noticed Hughes standing in the doorway with her gun aimed at the two of them. The look of shock and hurt on his face immediately switched to bitter resentment. "No."

"Sorry, boss," Hughes said with a shrug.

"Why?" Parker asked as he struggled to his feet.

"I could give you some story about disillusionment and disgust," Hughes said, "but I respect you too much for that. It was the money. Lowell offered me quite a nice little stipend to get me to switch sides. Now, why don't you two stand next to each other so I can finish off the job the pretty lady there couldn't manage to do."

Weiss moved over to Parker as he had been instructed. The poor guy was having trouble standing on his own feet, but Weiss couldn't help him out. He was too busy trying to make sure that Hughes didn't notice him fumbling in his pocket for the second vial. But Hughes was checking to make sure that Sydney was really out cold and she couldn't keep an eye on all three of them.

"Can someone at least explain what just happened here?" Parker asked. "I'd like to know why I'm about to die."

"Caryn?" Weiss said, figuring she didn't deserve the respect of being called by her last name any longer.

"It's about moving up in the world," Hughes said. "Hitching your wagon to a star and all that."

"Well that clears things up perfectly," Parker said. "And how long have you been hitching your wagon to this particular star?"

"Since before you and I ever met," Hughes said. "So don't worry. It wasn't anything you ever did. The wheels were in motion before you took over the team."

"So for the past few years, every failure we ever had?"

"I made happen," Hughes said. There was a noticeable amount of pride in her voice, but Weiss could tell that it was mixed with a small amount of regret. He suspected that regret might be an opening to exploit, then realized that Parker—battered and beaten Parker—was already doing just that.

"And the lab location?" Parker asked. "You were the one who found the lab and brought it to my attention."

"Lowell gave it to me to give to you," she said, "in case you ever started getting too close. If that day ever came, I was supposed to give you the information to get inside."

"And what would I find in there?" he asked with growing anger that he could clearly no longer contain. "What are McCormack and Dobbs going to find in there?"

"There are some things I prefer not to ask," she said.

Parker could barely manage to shake his head. "You mean prefer not to think about. Does it make you feel better, not having to deal with the fact that you've sent McCormack and Dobbs to their deaths?

And what about me? How are you going to justify killing me to yourself? Because that's what you're going to have to do if you even want to think about getting out of here alive yourself."

"Don't worry, Trent," she said. "I may have to kill you, but I'll let you live the longest. These two Homeland Security agents get to go first."

She raised her gun at Weiss. Even with the distraction Parker had unwittingly provided, Weiss still hadn't managed to attach the vial to the injector. It was too hard to manipulate with only one hand jammed into his pocket.

"Good-bye," she said with the most pleasant look Weiss had seen on her face since he had met her.

Weiss finally gave up all pretense of hiding what he was up to. He pulled the items from his pocket and used both hands to slip the vial into the injector just as Hughes fired. Before Weiss could react, Agent Parker threw his body in front of the bullet.

As Parker dropped in front of him, Weiss flung the injector at Hughes. He could hear it slice through the air as it found its target, embedding itself squarely in her shoulder. As she raised her left hand to pull out the needle, the gun dropped from her right. A moment later, she fell to the floor, unconscious. Weiss didn't bother to catch her before she landed on the hardwood.

Weiss looked down at Parker. He was bleeding from the shoulder, but there was no time to tend to him. Weiss turned to the computer instead. He saw the screen had returned to the live video feed. The back of Nadia's head filled the monitor, indicating that the feed wasn't the only thing with some life still in it. Nadia had just pulled up her mask and was turning toward Vaughn with a confused look on her beautiful face.

Weiss flew across the room in three bounding steps. He reached for the microphone and screamed his orders into it. "Houdini to Shotgun. Abort mission! Do you hear me? Abort! Abort!"

CHAPTER 17

TORONTO

Nadia took point as Vaughn punched the access code into the lock on the warehouse's exterior door. Once he hit the final digit, they all heard the locking mechanism disengage with a loud click. For the first time all night, Nadia saw a smile coming through the mask on McCormack's face. He may not have wanted to share the glory with her and Vaughn, but it was clear that the guy was thrilled that Lowell was about to get his comeuppance. Nadia couldn't blame him for his happiness. He had invested a lot of time to get to this night.

Vaughn carefully pulled the door open as Nadia aimed her gun inside. The immediate path was clear, so she waved them all forward. One by one, they entered the warehouse. McCormack was in the lead, while she and Vaughn followed, and Dobbs took up the rear. She wasn't thrilled by the configuration. It made her feel like she was under the guys' protection. But since she and Vaughn were the only ones who knew the real mission, they needed to be covered at all times.

They met no resistance in the entry hall. The inside of the building didn't look like a typical warehouse with a big open space. Makeshift rooms lined the hall as if someone had converted the space into the saddest-looking office building ever. The hallway and the rooms were dark and empty. They hadn't come across any of the workers yet, but she knew they had to be there. The last smoke break had ended a half hour earlier. Vaughn and Dodd had watched them all go back in through the door. Nadia hadn't expected the place to be buzzing with activity, but she didn't think it would seem so deserted.

The team quickly moved toward the back of the warehouse. Marshall's signal jammer was running out of time. Nadia hadn't seen any surveillance cameras since they entered the building, but she knew they couldn't risk assuming there were none around. Considering Lowell's rumored penchant for security, there had to be cameras in the area. Once security saw them on the monitors, she expected people would start coming out of the woodwork.

Then again, that was another thing that was bugging Nadia. When the cameras outside went dark, she had expected at least one of the guards to come check on the main door. It should have been standard operating procedure even if they thought it was just a glitch in the system. What Lowell had been storing in that warehouse was worth extra precaution as far as she was concerned. And yet, no one was coming to greet them.

"I don't like this," she whispered to Vaughn.

"You're not the only one," he replied.

Vaughn waved them forward and the foursome double-timed it through the hall. They were still careful to check every room, but knew they were up against some kind of clock, whether real or imagined. When they finally passed the last small office, they found themselves in the storage part of the warehouse. But instead of shelves full of Sway and a lab with researchers making more of the drug, they found nothing but a big, dark empty space.

Curiouser and curiouser, Nadia thought as she searched the area for any signs of life. Eventually her eyes dropped to the floor where she did find at least one thing of interest. Nadia was apparently the first to see it. She lifted her flashlight from her pack and aimed it at the floor. A four-by-three-foot hatch was sitting a few yards in front of them. As a group, they hurried to the hole and looked inside, careful to lead with their guns. There was nothing down there except a staircase leading down to a tunnel.

At first Nadia thought that they had triggered an alarm that had sent the workers scurrying as soon as Vaughn had opened the door. But that didn't explain the lack of equipment and boxes of Sway. Even if every person in the place had grabbed something on the way out, there was no way they could have cleared out the place that quickly—unless the warehouse never had anything in it in the first place.

Nadia lifted her mask and turned to Vaughn. She was about to ask if they should bother going down into the tunnel when she heard Weiss's voice yelling in her ear.

Houdini to Shotgun. Abort mission! Do you hear me? Abort! Abort!

Nadia dropped the flashlight and bolted back to the front entrance without bothering to wait for Vaughn to relay the order they had all heard. She could feel the men on her heels. She didn't know what she was running from or why, but she knew she had to move.

Running faster than she ever had before, Nadia blew past the empty offices, not even stopping to make sure that someone wasn't going to spring out at her. It didn't matter. No one was there. That much was clear. They had all gone a half hour earlier, clearing the way for whatever was about to happen.

Nadia could see the door in front of her when she heard the first of the explosions tear through the building.

She ran even faster, though she didn't know how it was possible. Vaughn passed her and reached the door first, pushing it open and keeping it clear for the rest of the team. Explosions continued to rock the building as they ran out. Once

McCormack cleared the doorway, Vaughn let go of the door and rejoined them in their run. They barely made it across the parking lot when the building finally went up entirely, knocking them all to the ground.

"Shotgun! Evergreen! Are you all right?" Weiss's voice echoed in Nadia's head. "Evergreen! Answer me." Her head rolled to the side. She had been expecting to see Weiss standing beside her. He sounded so close. *But why isn't he calling me by my name?*

"Evergreen!"

Nadia's mind cleared with the imagined force of another explosion. Weiss wasn't beside her. He was hundreds of miles away. She shook off her confusion and pulled herself up off the ground. "This is Evergreen," she said into the air. "I'm okay."

"Good, Evergreen," Weiss replied. She could hear the relief in his voice. "Oh, you don't know how good your voice sounds right now. What's the status of Shotgun and the others?"

Nadia took a second to get her bearings. The warehouse she had been inside mere seconds ago no longer existed. Bodies were littered around her. She feared they were all dead. McCormack was the closest to her. She was relieved to hear he was groaning, much like he had been in response to every question she had asked earlier in the evening. He would be fine.

Nadia moved over to Dobbs. He was bleeding profusely from a head wound. But those types of wounds tended to bleed heavily, regardless of severity. He wasn't moaning, but she could tell he was breathing. By the time she checked his pulse—rapid, but steady—she saw that Vaughn was already getting up.

"Everyone's more or less okay," she replied. "Battered, but okay."

"Thank you," Weiss said. It sounded like he was directing that thanks to some higher power instead of her.

And it was just then that the voice of a higher power of a different kind came over the comm. "Houdini, report," Sloane's voice said from his position at APO headquarters. "What the hell is going on out there?"

Weiss's blood ran cold. His mission had literally exploded in their faces, or behind their backs, depending on one's perspective. Sydney was unconscious. The lead DEA agent was barely alive. His second officer had betrayed them all. Dixon was missing. And the rest of the team was badly injured. Weiss couldn't have done any worse if he had planned it that way.

"Houdini!" Sloane repeated. Marshall must have run to get Sloane when he heard the mission fall apart over the comm. Weiss would have to remember to thank Marshall for that someday. And he was already enjoying images of the ways he would find to do just that.

At the moment, Weiss wished he was his illusionist ancestor and namesake so that he could disappear. But he knew that was the coward's way out. He also knew that it was physically impossible. And even if it wasn't, he knew that Sloane would manage to hunt him down anyway.

Weiss summoned his courage and gave Sloane a full report on what he knew had transpired, combined with what he assumed had happened. He didn't editorialize. He didn't crack wise. He just presented the facts, clearly and concisely, letting the chips fall where they may.

There was a long silence on the other end of the comm when he was finished. He knew that

Nadia could hear that silence as well. He had just proven to her father that he, Eric Weiss, was exactly the kind of screwup he had probably been expected to be. But the thing was, Weiss didn't care. Dixon was still MIA. Lowell's lab was still in operation. And as far as Weiss was concerned, he still had a job to do.

Parker was slowly regaining consciousness on the floor beside him. While Weiss was giving his report to Sloane, he'd also managed to slow the DEA agent's bleeding with a compress. The bullet had gone cleanly through the shoulder. As far as Weiss could tell, the young agent would recover. But it was seeing the man's eyes flit open that gave Weiss the answer he had been looking for.

Weiss finally broke the silence himself, calling out to the microphone. "I know things look bad at the moment. But I've got an idea."

"Correct me if I'm wrong," Sloane said, "but it was one of your ideas that got us into this mess in the first place."

"Then imagine the beautiful symmetry of having one of my ideas get us out of it," Weiss said before he even realized he was talking back to Arvin Sloane. He suspected that people had been tortured and killed for much less in the man's considerably dark past, but he couldn't worry about that at the moment. "Merlin, are you there?"

There was a short pause. "Me?" Marshall asked. "Oh . . . yes. I'm sorry. I was just . . . are you aware that your mike's on and we could all hear what you just said?"

"Merlin!"

Weiss could practically hear him snap to attention. "Right! What do you need?"

He pulled the small metal box over to him. "These drugs you gave me. Which is the most powerful truth serum?"

"Red cap," Marshall said. "But use it sparingly. Too much can kill a person."

"And the one in the silver cap immediately revives a person from the sedative?" he asked.

"Yes," Marshall replied. "Otherwise they'll need to complete one full REM cycle before they can wake and be expected to function properly. It's an unfortunate side effect of the sedative, which, I guess, is not so much a side effect as it is an *effect,* since it's a sedative and all."

"Thanks, Merlin," Weiss said. "That's all I need to know."

"But I think . . . I think I only put one of the psychostimulants in the pack," Marshall continued. "I know. Poor planning on my part, but—"

"It's okay, Marshall. I'm only going to need one," Weiss said.

"Fine," Sloane said, getting back on the line. "Revive Phoenix and then go and retrieve Outrigger."

"Sorry, sir," Weiss said. "Can't do that. I need to speak to the DEA turncoat first."

"Negative," Sloane said. "I am now placing Phoenix in charge of this mission. Your orders are to wake her and let me speak to her so we can get this back on track."

"No can do," Weiss said, unable to believe the words coming out of his own mouth. "Even if Phoenix is conscious, she won't know how to safely get back onto Lowell's compound. And she could still be under the effects of Sway. My guess is that she's going to need that full REM cycle to sleep off the drug, like Malcolm Norwood had suggested."

"Um . . . sir," Marshall's hesitant voice came over the comm, "he's got a point . . . sir. I think it's possible that Phoenix will need that cycle for the drug to clear her system."

"How long will that take?" Sloane asked.

"Um . . . approximately ninety minutes, sir," Marshall said.

"Outrigger could be dead by then," Sloane said.

"With all due respect, sir," Weiss said, "Outrigger could already be dead. But if Phoenix and I go in there while she's still under the effects of Sway, we will all be dead."

This time, there was a long silence over the intercom. It was killing Weiss to know that he had an audience of Nadia, Vaughn, Marshall, and assorted DEA agents listening to him argue with his boss.

Finally Sloane's voice broke through the silence. "You may proceed."

CHAPTER 18

"You sure you're going to be all right?" Weiss asked Parker as he propped the guy up on one of the kitchen chairs that he had pulled over to the couch.

"Well, I've had the crap beaten out of me and I think I'm still bleeding slightly from a gunshot wound," Parker said, leaning on the edge of the couch for support, "so 'all right' may be a bit of an overstatement. But I don't think I'm going to die."

"Good to hear," Weiss said as he moved back to the kitchen table and injected the diluted truth serum into Hughes's system. Marshall had walked him through the process of cutting down the drug he had taken out of the metal box. Weiss was pretty sure he got it right, but he'd find out soon enough. He knew he was taking a risk with this plan, but he had already committed to it, so there was really no turning back now.

Weiss checked to make sure that the ropes tying Hughes to her chair were tight before he loaded the second vial into the injector. He wished he could call an ambulance to tend to Parker, but he didn't have the comfort of time to let anyone compromise the scene. No matter what kind of magic Sloane could work to insist that local law enforcement not interfere with their mission, any EMT that came across a house where one person was out cold, another was tied to a chair, and a third was beaten and shot . . . well, there were going to be questions—questions that would stall his rescue.

"Sylvia really didn't mean to attack you like that," Weiss said reassuringly, for the third time since Parker had regained consciousness. "Things were out of her control."

"I get it," Parker said, "even if I don't get what's

going on. I believe what you're saying about her. But please, don't treat me like I'm still supposed to believe her name is Sylvia. I'm pretty sure you guys aren't from Homeland Security, either. When we start injecting people with drugs to force information out of them without bothering to get permission from anyone first, I'm thinking we're walking on some shaky legal ground here. There's something a little *unsanctioned* about this whole thing."

Weiss tried to think of ways to play off the comment as he loaded the injector with the psychostimulant. Parker had already been through so much today—not the least of which being Hughes's betrayal—that it seemed unfair to lie to him any longer. Still, Weiss couldn't admit to what was really going on. Divulging APO's existence would be giving Sloane a reason to kill Weiss, for sure. But he had to give the guy *something*. Parker had earned at least a partial truth.

Weiss stopped what he was doing. "Obviously I can't tell you all the things you want to hear," Weiss said. "But I will say that we *are* the good guys, that Lowell needs to be stopped because he's dabbling in some very dangerous things, and that I am going to need your help to do it."

Parker seemed to be considering what Weiss had said. Either that or he was just focusing on trying to remain conscious. "What do you need from me?" Parker said as he stood tall and walked over to Weiss and Hughes at the table.

"The drug I've given Hughes should force her to tell us the truth," Weiss said. "But considering how she feels about me, it might be easier to get it from her if she hears a friendly voice."

"And lord knows she and I are such good buddies," Parker scoffed. His statement was filled with understandable bitterness over the fact that she had lied to him and had been undermining the DEA's operation since the start.

"Yeah, but she was going to kill you last, so that means she likes you more than the rest of us," Weiss joked, finally getting some of his old reliable humor back. It helped that he was starting to think positively again. They could do this.

Weiss wasn't sure if Parker had smiled or his lips had just tightened due to a twinge of pain. "Let me at her."

"Oh good," Weiss said. "Productive rage. I can work with that." He jabbed the injector into Hughes's neck, flooding the woman's system with the psychostimulant. Her body stiffened and she immediately awoke, sucking in a deep gasp of breath.

"Good morning, sunshine," Weiss said as he checked to make sure she was conscious. Her eyes were glazed over and lacking focus. Weiss wasn't sure if that was due to the truth serum, the sedative, the drug he had given her to counteract the sedative, or some combination thereof. Either way, he couldn't help but find a new respect for the thought that had gone into the development of Sway. If Sydney had returned from Lowell's compound looking like Hughes looked on the drugs she was on—with bleary eyes and a vacant expression—Weiss would have been onto Sydney in a second.

"Go to hell," Hughes said groggily.

"Someone's not a morning person," Weiss said in a singsong voice. "Agent Parker, I'm sure you know what to do here."

"Yes," Parker said somberly as he stepped up to Hughes. "Hello, Caryn. I'm going to ask you some questions and you're going to give us some answers. I think I deserve the truth from you right about now."

Hughes sat in stony silence.

"First, has Lowell killed the other Homeland Security agent?" Parker asked.

Hughes tried to look away from him, as if eye contact was necessary for the drug to work. Her head lolled slightly to the side and she still lacked focus. But she did manage to speak after a moment's hesitation. "No, he wants to get information from the guy first."

Weiss tried not to allow the sudden fear to register on his face. Even though he was glad to learn that Dixon was alive, it was not all good news. The kinds of things Dixon could admit to while under the influence of Sway were gold to a man like Lowell. If one set of stolen FBI files had gotten everyone in such a tizzy, Weiss was afraid to imagine what Dixon's level of clearance would provide for Lowell's organization.

"How long do we have before Lowell kills him?" Weiss prodded Parker to ask. The DEA agent leaned in and repeated the question.

"I don't know," was Hughes's response.

"I need to know about security," Weiss said, moving on to more active measures.

"Caryn," Parker prompted, "tell us everything you know about Lowell's compound. What kind of security does he have? How do we get past it?"

Hughes turned back to face him. Her eyes were still hazy and her expression was emotionless. "He's got half a dozen guards on at all times. Video cameras at various intervals around the property . . ." She trailed off.

"Go on," Weiss prodded.

"That's it," Hughes said. "Except for the electrical equipment inside the house."

Weiss moved in to take over. Not that Parker wasn't doing a fine job, but Weiss just couldn't sit back and watch any longer. He needed to move things along. "You're lying," he said. "All available intel indicates that his girlfriend designed some intensive lethal response system."

"That's the lie," Hughes slurred. "There's nothing."

"And you expect us to believe that?" Weiss asked, checking the vial to make sure the diluted solution had been administered fully. It had. *Maybe I did make a mistake while diluting it,* Weiss thought.

"It's the truth," Hughes said through the haze. "Who do you think provided the intel in the first place? Me."

Weiss looked to Parker, who nodded in confirmation.

"Lowell is all about the show," Hughes continued rambling. "He's always focused on reputation. What better way to keep people out than by fooling them into believing the place is impenetrable?"

"That's ridiculous," Parker said.

"Fooled you for a few years now," Hughes said mockingly.

"We've got satellite photos of construction at the compound," Parker said. "We've got shipping orders for weapons and other security-related items."

"Fakes," Hughes said. "I helped Felicia make them."

Parker looked stricken. It was one thing to know he had been betrayed. It was another to actually hear how the betrayal had been perpetrated over the years. He slumped down in the chair beside Hughes.

If Weiss hadn't been so angry, he would have been more upset over the news. In his mind, Weiss just upgraded Lowell to criminal genius. It was the most cost-effective and impressive security plan he had ever witnessed. Sydney and Dixon hadn't even needed to go in undercover. They could have just snuck into the compound on their own and made off with the information in the middle of the night. They had certainly gotten into way more secured facilities than Lowell's home. "Unbelievable," he said aloud.

Weiss looked to Parker. He couldn't imagine what the kid was going through right now. The levels of betrayal just kept deepening. David Lowell would have been an open-and-shut case if it weren't for the fact that Hughes was working against the DEA team the entire time. Eventually there would be a time to dwell on this revelation, but now was not that time.

"What about the real lab?" Weiss asked. "Where is Lowell developing his new drug?" He knew he was revealing too much to Parker by mentioning the drug, but the guy was probably piecing together things well enough on his own by now that Weiss didn't have to be too secretive about it.

Hughes's mouth broke into a lopsided smile. "Lowell makes a lot of drugs. Which one are you talking about?"

Weiss worried that her ability to be coy might

mean the serum was wearing off. Marshall had said something about temporary effects when he was walking Weiss through the dilution process. He still had enough of the undiluted drug to make up some more, but he wasn't sure Hughes's body could take any more chemicals at the moment. That being the case, Weiss knew he didn't have time to play her games. "Sway," he said. "Where is the lab that he's using to make Sway?"

"I don't know," she replied.

"Yes. You do," Weiss insisted.

"No. I don't," she replied forcefully while looking straight at him. Weiss could see that her eyes were beginning to clear. Either she was coming out of the effects of the drug and lying to him, or she was still telling him the truth. Weiss couldn't be sure.

"Parker, see if you can get anything else out of her," Weiss said as he picked up the laptop and took it to the other side of the room. He reported back to Sloane and the team in Toronto that they still didn't know about the lab, but it was likely that Dixon was alive. They were all just as shocked as Weiss had been earlier when he relayed the information about the lack of real security on the compound, none more so than Marshall, who expounded on the utter genius behind the simple plan for quite a while.

"When can you go in to retrieve Outrigger?" Sloane asked, getting the conversation back on track.

"Even with the lessened security, it's not a one-man job," Weiss reluctantly admitted. "We need to hit hard and fast or else Lowell could kill Outrigger before I can get to him."

"What about Parker?" Nadia asked over the comm.

"He's in no condition to mount a rescue," Weiss said. "I'm going to need to wait for Phoenix."

"How long do we have before she can be wakened?" Sloane asked.

Weiss checked his watch. "Almost an hour." He looked over at Sydney's sleeping form on the couch. Even after that hour, there was no guarantee that she wasn't still going to be a slave to Sway. He was taking a chance that Norwood's comment about "sleeping off the effects" referred to a single REM cycle. It could be that the victims required a full night of sleep for the drug to leave their systems entirely. The problem was that he might never really know. Weiss could walk back into Lowell's compound and all it would take was one word from the man to turn Sydney back into a dangerous threat.

It was a chance Weiss was going to have to take. He had no choice but to wait for Sydney to wake up.

CHAPTER 19

Sydney heard a voice calling to her through the darkness. . . . It was saying her name . . . No . . . It was her call sign . . . *Phoenix.* . . . The voice was familiar . . . warm. . . . It wasn't Vaughn, but someone that reminded her of him. . . . It was Eric. . . . Her mind filled with relief as she thought, *Eric is alive.* She hadn't killed him. *But why would I think I killed him?*

Suddenly everything came back to her with a jolt as her eyes popped open.

"Hello, sleepyhead." Weiss's bright and beaming

face was the first thing she saw looming above her. Sydney looked around, gathering her senses. She was on the couch in the DEA cabin. It was still night outside the window, though she couldn't tell how long she had been out. She was about to ask when her eyes fell on Agent Parker, causing her to cringe inwardly. He looked as if he had been beaten to within an inch of his life. She had done that. Sure, she was under the effects of Sway, but it had been her hands that had attacked him. She could still remember the feel of his body as it took the full force of her punches. Her own skin was bruised around her knuckles.

Parker was dabbing at a wound on his shoulder. Dried blood was caked around it, but it had closed. It looked bad though, like he had been shot. That part Sydney did not remember doing.

"I'm so sorry," she said. "I . . . wasn't myself."

"Sammy explained," Parker said with a nod to Weiss. "Though I'm pretty sure he left out a lot of the story—and his real name."

Sydney looked to Weiss, who nodded in confirmation. She knew she could speak freely enough, so long as she didn't get into specifics. That was when she noticed that Caryn Hughes was tied to a chair in the kitchen area. Sydney was dying to know what had happened while she was out, but first she felt the need to explain her actions.

"Lowell ordered me to kill both of you," she said, stating what was probably obvious at this point. "But he left the method up to me. I tried to do it in a way that would give you a chance to fight back." She tried to stand but stumbled. She almost fell back onto the couch, but managed to stay mostly erect. "There was no other way to stop myself. I knew you'd figure it out if I just gave you time."

Weiss leaned over to help steady her. "Next time just turn on the gas and let us smell it to alert us to the danger. It will save some bruising," he said.

"And maybe a gunshot or two," Parker added.

"I'm pretty sure I didn't do that," Sydney said. "But if I did, I'm even more sorry about it."

"It's okay. It wasn't you," Parker said reassuringly, though he still kept his distance.

"She did it." Weiss nodded in the direction of the kitchen. Sydney turned and saw Hughes looking angrier than Sydney had ever seen the woman in the little time they had known each other.

Considering Hughes had been the one to inject Sydney with Sway in the first place, she didn't feel the least bit of concern for the woman now.

"Hello," Hughes said brightly. "Why don't you do me a favor and finish the job? Kill them."

Weiss and Parker immediately braced for another fight, but Sydney felt no need to move against them. She waited to see if maybe her reactions had just slowed from being knocked out, but the helpless feeling of being a slave to her body never came. The relief flooded over her. "It's okay," she said. "I'm pretty sure the drug's worn off. I was instructed to only take commands from her, Lowell, and Felicia. I feel no urge to kill you at all. Well, no more than I usually do," she added with a smile.

"That's nice to hear," Weiss said as he relaxed noticeably. He then updated her on the situation and all that she had missed in the hour and a half she had been asleep. Sydney was glad to hear that Vaughn and Nadia were fine, but her concern for Dixon grew when she learned how long it had been since she had left him. On the bright side, she was glad—and more than a bit frustrated—to hear that Lowell's compound wasn't nearly as secure as they had originally been led to believe.

"But we're still outnumbered when it comes to guards," Sydney said. "And it's too risky to try to sneak in when we don't know where the cameras are placed."

"I had an idea about that while you were out," Weiss said as he turned back to Hughes. "She's going to help us."

"Like hell I am," Hughes said.

In response, Weiss held up his gun. "Oh, I think you are."

A few minutes later, Sydney found herself in the passenger's seat of the rental car holding her own gun on Caryn Hughes while the hostage sat on the driver's side in control of the car. Sydney knew it was risky putting her behind the wheel, but it was the only way to get back inside Lowell's compound. Meanwhile Weiss was in the backseat with the medical injector filled with the last of the tranquilizer vials in case Hughes got out of hand. They had all agreed it was best for Parker to stay behind and call for an ambulance. Aside from the fact that he wouldn't be of much help in his current state, Parker had held off going to the hospital long enough.

"We're almost there," Sydney said to Weiss.

With a nod, he slipped down to the floor. It was a tight fit, but he needed to stay out of sight. If anyone saw them coming in, they might not question why Hughes would return with Sydney. But there was no way they would ignore someone else in the car.

"Stick to the script," Sydney said as she pressed the gun into Hughes's side. The woman glared at Sydney out of the corner of her eye but continued on to the gate. Hughes pulled up beside the intercom and rolled down the window.

"Welcome back," the same disembodied voice from earlier said to Hughes. "Why'd you bring *her* back with you?"

"She's got some information Lowell needs to hear," Hughes said. "Let us in."

Once again, the voice didn't bother to respond, but the gate opened allowing them access to the grounds. Sydney saw the two perimeter guards watch the car as they pulled down the road. Counting off the two guards inside the gate, two at the front of the house, and one stationed wherever the other end of that intercom was placed, that left seven guards unaccounted for, if Hughes was to be believed about the guard count. As long as the guards didn't rush them at once, Sydney knew that she and Weiss could hold them all off long enough to save Dixon—so long as it wasn't already too late.

"Slow down," Sydney said to Hughes. Their speed was ticking up noticeably as they blew through the grounds. "I said, slow down!" she commanded as she pressed the gun deeper into Hughes's side.

"Go ahead and shoot me," Hughes said, and she slammed on the gas, throwing Sydney back in her seat.

"Hughes!" Weiss yelled as he popped up in the back. "Stop the car!"

"Okay," she said as she took a sharp turn. The tires squealed as she hit the brakes and sent the car into a spin. Sydney grabbed for the door as she struggled to hold the gun on Hughes. After a second revolution, the car slipped off the road and the back end slammed into a tree.

Sydney was thrown against her seatbelt as the car banged to a stop. She felt the weight of Weiss's body thrown into the back of her seat as the injector flew forward and landed on the floor in front of her. She hoped he was okay back there, since he hadn't had a seatbelt on.

As soon as the car had come to a stop, Hughes unbuckled her seatbelt and threw open the driver's side door. Sydney quickly exchanged the gun for the injector and—taking a page out of Weiss's playbook—threw the injector into Hughes's back as she tried to make her escape. A second later, the woman slumped back into the seat.

"You okay?" Sydney asked as she freed herself from the seatbelt that had dug into her skin.

"More or less," Weiss said, massaging his jaw. "Is she out?"

Sydney removed the injector. The vial of sedative was empty. "She's out."

"Poor woman has more drugs in her system than a patient of Dr. Kevorkian," Weiss said. Then he added, "Good." For good measure, he took a zip tie out of his pocket and bound her arms to the steering wheel.

"We've got to move," Sydney said as they both threw open their doors. "Security must have heard the crash."

As if in response, a bullet shattered the window of the door Sydney was holding onto. She immediately ducked down, grabbing her gun off the seat beside her.

"I think you're right," Weiss yelled back to her. He had taken up position behind his own door. The two guards from the gate were coming up on them. They'd probably alerted the rest of the team by now. Pretty soon a dozen guards would converge on the area from all around the compound. She and Weiss were going to have to take them out quickly if they were going to save Dixon and take care of David Lowell.

Dixon wished he could stop himself. He had tried using every resistance technique at his disposal. At first, he refused to speak at all. But Lowell's commands had forced him to answer the questions. Dixon was amazed by the effectiveness of Sway. It was quite possibly the most insidious drug he had ever heard of, much less experienced firsthand. He was defenseless against Lowell's questioning, no matter the amount of training he had received over the years to resist brainwashing. The drug undid all that in a matter of seconds.

The interrogation had begun innocently enough, if not in the most timely manner. A few minutes after Sydney and Hughes had left the house, Felicia and Lowell had gone off for a private discussion. While they were gone, Dixon tried to break free of the chair, but it was much sturdier than he had imagined. All that he had managed to do was bruise himself and his ego.

Dixon had assumed that he had received a brief reprieve when he heard a car drive away from the house. It didn't seem likely that his captors would leave him unattended, but there was no telling what kind of false sense of security Lowell's ego would allow. But Lowell soon returned to the room and made good on his promise to conduct a few phone calls before he got to work questioning Dixon. It was insulting. Lowell was intentionally treating Dixon like he wasn't even important enough to warrant an immediate interrogation. Of course that was before Lowell knew all that Dixon had to offer.

Even more offensive had been the fact that Lowell didn't even bother to make his business calls in private. He made them right in front of Dixon as if teasing the man with his pending death. There was no way Lowell would leave Dixon alive after what he had heard on those calls. Not like Dixon had any doubt about Lowell's plan from the start.

After Lowell had finished his last call, he finally returned his attention to his prisoner. Dixon had joked that the man could have at least turned him around to enjoy the view of Lake Superior at night. Lowell had responded by turning on some classical music for Dixon to enjoy while the criminal went to work.

Throughout the evening Lowell had refused to get too close to Dixon. Lowell was armed, but without his people there to protect him, he made sure to keep his distance. He had only moved close to Dixon once since Felicia had left. And that was to inject Dixon with a dose of Sway before backing off for the questioning.

Still under the impression that Dixon worked with the United States Department of Homeland Security, Lowell was most interested in what the organization had already known about him. Dixon was smart enough to craft his responses in such a way that he answered all of Lowell's questions without giving away too much information. That all changed when Dixon was forced into revealing his true identity.

"So, your name isn't Chris Soto, like Hughes told me?" Lowell had asked.

"No."

"Then what is it?"

"Marcus R. Dixon."

"Interesting. And, just out of curiosity, Marcus R. Dixon, do you actually work for Homeland Security?"

"No."

It only took a few more questions to wrestle the name APO out of Dixon's unwilling mouth. From there, it was like the floodgates had been opened and Dixon was forced to spill out everything he knew about the organization, its history, and the history of its core members. Lowell was practically beside himself with glee, especially when he heard all about the checkered history of noted humanitarian Arvin Sloane. It was like Lowell had discovered a new hero to model his own life after, all thanks to the information Dixon was providing.

Dixon knew he was sealing the fate of the black ops organization and of his friends. If the public would be outraged to learn the government had been developing a drug like Sway, he could only imagine what would happen when Lowell leaked word of the existence of APO and the true history of its leader, Arvin Sloane. Not that Dixon cared about Sloane, but he did worry about the effects it would have on the rest of the team, most notably Nadia.

Dixon wished he could do anything to stop the flow of information. With every word, he was betraying his friends and destroying their cause. Sloane wasn't the only one with secrets that would cost him. At one time or another almost every member of the APO team had been forced into making judgment calls that could be easily questioned if the truth came out. Dixon was going through hell, all while Schubert's *Ave Maria* played softly in the background.

"So you're actually now working for a man who killed your wife?" Lowell asked for a second time. He was clearly enjoying himself and impressed with everything he continued to learn about Arvin Sloane.

"Yes," Dixon said, without bothering to go into detail as to why.

"This Sloane is amazing," Lowell said in awe. "I've got to meet him sometime."

"I'm sure something can be arranged," Dixon said.

"You know," Lowell said, "you're pretty funny."

"I try," Dixon said, right before he heard the

gunshots. It sounded like automatic fire. It was still off in the distance, but it was moving closer. Lowell looked more surprised than Dixon felt. He had never doubted that Sydney would get him out of this. "Looks like someone's going to give you the chance to meet Arvin Sloane very soon," Dixon said with a laugh.

Lowell rushed to his desk and picked up one of the secured phones. He only pressed one button before shouting "What the hell's going on?" into the receiver.

As one of the security guards updated Lowell on his situation, Dixon realized he now had his chance. He had been thinking of escape routes while Lowell had made his earlier calls, but nothing had come at the time. It was Lowell's own showmanship that had finally inspired Dixon. He just needed Lowell to get a bit closer.

Lowell slammed down the phone. "It looks like your friend is more resourceful than I gave her credit for," he said as he paced behind the desk, trying to figure out what to do. Considering how insulated Lowell had been in his criminal career, Dixon doubted that he had ever come under direct attack before. He probably had no clue how to defend himself. And with Felicia gone on whatever mission she had been sent on, Lowell was probably even more ineffectual.

This would all work nicely to Dixon's advantage.

"May I suggest letting me go?" Dixon said, still aware of the fact that he had to be careful what he said while he was under the effects of Sway.

"Oh, I'll let you go all right," Lowell said as he moved toward Dixon. "I'll let you go take care of your friends for me, save my security the trouble."

Dixon was pleased to note that Lowell was telescoping his plan but not actually giving a direct order. That would work to Dixon's benefit. He only needed a few seconds to get to safety.

Under fear of attack, Lowell was bold enough to holster his gun and approach Dixon, yet distracted enough not to think to warn his prisoner to stay still. Pleased by that small bit of luck, Dixon clamped his fists onto the ends of the armchair. The high-backed chair was going to be cumbersome, but it wasn't that heavy. It was just weighty enough to do some serious damage.

As soon as Lowell bent to unlock the cuffs, Dixon struck.

Planting his feet together on the ground, Dixon

pushed up and stood as best as he could, pulling the chair up with him. Using the full force of his legs, Dixon bent forward and sent his skull crashing into Lowell's stomach. Lowell's gun fell onto the floor as he stumbled and tripped backward over the star-shaped coffee table. His head banged against the edge of the couch as he crumpled to the ground.

Lowell wasn't out, but he was disoriented. Dixon suspected that another good blow might do the trick, but with the chair strapped to him, it was too hard to maneuver into the space between the coffee table and couch. And if Lowell gathered his senses too quickly and barked out a command, it would all be over.

The gun had landed at Dixon's feet. He tried to reach for it, but it was much too awkward to try to bend with the chair to reach it. When all else failed, he gave the gun a good, solid kick, sending it sailing across the floor, into the bathroom and out of the mix.

Instead of going for Lowell, Dixon hiked the chair up on his back and ran for the state of the art stereo system playing the classical music. Once there, he sat back down in the chair to get his hand at the level it needed to be for what had to be done. From out of the corner of his eye, Dixon could see Lowell struggling to his feet. Ignoring the man, Dixon turned the volume knob on the stereo all the way to its highest setting.

Dixon had correctly anticipated that Lowell would have spent his money on the best equipment available. There wasn't much in the way of electronics in the house, but what was there would be the best. The stereo was no different. The highest volume setting sent out music that was crisp and clear and absolutely deafening, more than loud enough to drown out any command Lowell would try to yell.

Once the music was set, Dixon turned toward Lowell. There was real fear in the man's eyes as he tried to shout orders to Dixon. As suspected, his voice simply could not carry over the blasting sounds.

It was a standoff. Dixon stood between Lowell and the door. Even though he was strapped to a high-backed leather chair, Dixon knew that he was in control of this situation. It was likely that Lowell had never been forced into a physical confrontation before. With his lack of experience, Lowell tried to do exactly what Dixon had anticipated: He made a run for the door.

Using just what he had at his disposal, Dixon turned himself quickly as Lowell tried to bolt past him. The chair swung around Dixon's body, pulling his arm with it as the wooden piece slammed into Lowell and sent him stumbling back several steps, finally falling on his ass. Dixon's right arm had been wrenched in the move, but he was still able to lift the chair with it. As experienced as he was in hand-to-hand combat, Dixon knew the chair would have to go if he wanted to get out of this before security came to help. The guards must have all been distracted by the gunfire Dixon had heard earlier, but they were bound to turn up soon.

While Lowell was struggling to get back to his feet, Dixon slammed the chair against the wall, hoping to smash it without doing harm to his own body. It didn't work. He tried two more times with little to show for it. He could feel the chair straining at its joints, but it was one of the more formidably made pieces of furniture he had ever come across.

Lowell was up again. His anger apparently outweighed his good senses as he decided to charge

Dixon directly. That move went about as well as Dixon had thought it would. All it took was for Dixon to bend forward and slide the chair up to send the wooden top of the high-back into Lowell's jaw.

This time, Dixon did hear Lowell's howl of rage over the deafening music as the man screamed in pain and anger. It didn't matter, though. Lowell would never be able to use that anger to properly fuel his fight. Even with a chair strapped to him, Dixon was still the one in charge.

Lowell's mouth was gushing blood and his eyes were burning with fury that did not match his abilities. It was clear that he thought he was about to go in for the kill. But he didn't realize where the fight had taken him. Dixon tried to shout a warning, but it was no use. Even if Lowell could hear him, the man was way past listening. Lowell charged at Dixon one last time.

Seeing the move coming a mile away, Dixon braced himself as Lowell's body slammed into his. All it took was a good kick to knock Lowell off-balance and send him crashing through the huge picture window. The man's body was gone before Dixon could even tell if Lowell had realized what had happened.

Dixon breathed a deep sigh of relief as he looked out the window. Through the tree branches, he could see Lowell's twisted and broken body lying on the ground below; he had fallen into the wash of light from one of the security posts. Dixon couldn't help but think the man had been wrong when he brought them into the room earlier. The view from the window wasn't spectacular at all.

When Dixon turned back around, he was surprised to see the door standing open. It was understandable that he hadn't heard anyone come into the room with the classical music still blaring. Thankfully, it wasn't security that had come for him. It was Weiss and Sydney.

CHAPTER 20

"Are you okay?" Sydney asked after she turned off the stereo.

"More or less," Dixon said as he sat in the chair he was still bound to by the handcuffs. "Just be careful what you say around me at the moment."

Weiss got a mischievous look on his face but stayed businesslike. "I'd ask where Lowell went, but I think I've got my answer," he said as he crossed to the smashed picture window. "Hope he didn't have the keys to those cuffs on him, because they're going to be hard to find in what's left of him."

Sydney cringed at the thought of the image but didn't bother to look. "I'll check Felicia's desk," she said as she did just that. Sydney found a small set of keys that looked like they belonged to the handcuffs in exactly the same spot from which Felicia had taken them to undo Sydney's restraints a little more than two hours earlier. She then went over and released Dixon from the chair. "Where is Felicia?" she asked.

"I'm fairly certain she left soon after you did," Dixon said as he rubbed his now free wrists. She could tell that he was sore all over just by looking at him.

"Any idea where she went?" Weiss asked.

"Possibly," Dixon said, "but I think his computer might tell us for sure. Syd, do you still have the hard drive downloading device?"

"Right here," Sydney said as she pulled the small cigarette case out of her jacket pocket and moved over to Lowell's desk. She held the small metal box beside the hard drive as she woke the sleeping computer. As soon as the device went active, an alarm went off on Felicia's desk. The APO agents simply ignored it.

While Marshall's toy downloaded Lowell's files,

Sydney dug around the computer to see if she could find the location of the mystery lab. If it was in fact located in Toronto, Vaughn and Nadia's team was still intact and waiting for further instructions. They could potentially finish the job they had set out to do. However, Sydney suspected that, like everything else that evening, nothing they had known about the lab was true.

"Doesn't look like the DEA guys are going to be able to put Lowell on trial for his crimes," Weiss said. "Parker's not going to like that. Then again, I figure the poor guy is just ready for this op to be over, no matter what the result."

Sydney nodded her head in agreement, then saw a file that looked promising and clicked it open. "Once we go over these files and clean out anything too sensitive, we'll forward the rest of the information to him. At least he can close down all of Lowell's holdings before someone else takes over."

"That someone would be Felicia," Weiss said. "But somehow I don't think we're done with her yet."

"Me neither," Sydney said as she realized she had hit pay dirt. "Just what I thought. Lowell's lab isn't in Toronto. It's out here, only a couple of miles away."

Neither of the men looked surprised in the least at this point. "Felicia is probably there clearing out the stock," Weiss said. "She strikes me as the type to prepare for any contingency."

"Do you think you're okay to come with us?" Sydney asked Dixon. Having experienced the effects of Sway firsthand, Sydney knew it didn't affect him physically. All the same, she would prefer that Dixon lay low until it wore off.

Thankfully, he agreed. "I don't think it's safe," he said. "No telling what anyone could force me to do. What's the status of security here?"

"Everyone had been subdued," Weiss said. "The compound is secure. Although Caryn Hughes might wake up in about an hour and a half. Until then, maybe you should wait here while we finish up, catch a few z's yourself."

"I don't expect that this would be a good place to rest," Dixon said. "But I'll keep an eye on the place."

Sydney wasn't exactly thrilled with the plan, but they couldn't waste any time. They needed to get to the lab before the stock of Sway was lost to them. It was entirely possible that Felicia had been alerted to what had just happened at the compound. She might be on her way back at the moment, but it was more likely that she was preparing to make sure Lowell's empire continued, even if he was captured. There was no way she could know he was dead yet since the guards had all been taken out before that happened. No one was left to inform her, as far as Sydney could tell.

"Wait," Sydney said as she stepped up to Dixon and looked him right in the eyes. "You are not to take orders from anyone from this point forward."

"Thank you, Syd," Dixon said. She could personally understand the relief he felt in receiving that command.

"Hey, wait up," Weiss said lightly. "I'm still in charge of this mission. He has to take orders from me."

"Not even if I was on all the Sway in the world," Dixon joked.

The three shared a laugh before Sydney and Weiss left the office. Considering the rental car was fairly useless at this point, they hotwired Lowell's convertible Lexus and borrowed it to take them to the lab. Weiss let out a loud whoop as he peeled out of the driveway.

"Good thing we got that extra insurance," Weiss said as he drove them past the wrecked rental car and Caryn's still unconscious body.

The lab was a straight shot down Route 11, back toward town. It would only take a couple of minutes to get there—less, the way Weiss was driving. When they passed the DEA cabin, they saw that the ambulance had arrived and Parker was being tended to. Sydney still felt bad for beating him so thoroughly, but there was nothing she could do about that at the moment but live with the regret.

Sydney checked the guns she had pulled off the security guards to make sure she and Weiss were properly armed for this new phase of their mission. In the meantime, Weiss called Vaughn on his cell phone and told the team to stand down. There was nothing left for them to do in Toronto.

Weiss continued to weave in and out around the few cars on the road. It was late enough that they didn't have any problems maintaining their speed. The only thing they had to worry about was being stopped by the police, but they each had more than enough false credentials on them to talk their way out of any situation. Luckily they didn't need to do any talking. They were at the lab in only a few minutes with no interruptions or flashing lights in the rearview.

Unlike the warehouse where Vaughn and Nadia had set up their stakeout, the real lab was located at a small business park. It made total sense that Lowell's illegal enterprises would look just as legitimate as his front businesses. The man really was all about the show.

Considering it was the middle of the night, it wasn't hard to find the illegal drug operation. A white panel truck was idling outside a building toward the rear of the business park and a handful of men were in the process of loading it with boxes. They looked like fairly generic workmen to Weiss, certainly not the same type of security personnel they had just encountered at Lowell's compound.

Weiss cut the car's headlights and pulled to the side of the road to watch the proceedings and scope out the area. Even from a distance, they could see Felicia was in charge of overseeing the move. Apparently they had arrived just in time. The last box was being loaded and the truck driver was closing the door and heading up to the cab of the truck with Felicia.

"What's the plan?" Sydney asked. By her estimation, there were about a half dozen men with Felicia. The building looked dark inside, so she doubted there was a night lab staff at work as they had been led to believe existed in the fake Toronto warehouse.

"We can't let that truck go," Weiss said as he revved the engine and peeled out toward the building.

What the plan lacked in stealth it made up for with the element of surprise. Felicia did look shocked to see Lowell's Lexus speeding toward them. She was even more surprised when the car was caught in the truck's headlights and she was able to see that Sydney and Weiss were inside. Sydney rolled down the window and aimed her gun at the truck, attempting to take out the tires before the driver could get away. Workmen scattered in every direction, taking cover as she fired.

"Hold on," Weiss said as he cut the wheel, turning the car perpendicular to the truck and blocking it in. The move sent her aim wild, causing her bullet to miss its intended target.

"Get down," Sydney said as she saw Felicia pull her own gun and start firing on the car. Sydney pulled on the seat control lever and dropped back into what little backseat there was so she could take a position at the window. When she looked up to take aim, she heard the truck's engine roar.

The sound of Felicia's voice yelling "Go!" exploded over the sound of the engine. Sydney barely had time to brace herself as the truck pulled out, clipping the back of the Lexus in the process. As the truck screeched past them, Sydney rose again to take stock of the situation. The hired hands were running off into the night. Apparently their pay grade didn't cover these types of situations. Felicia, however, had gone back into the building. Clearly her fight was not yet done.

"You go after Felicia," Weiss commanded. "I'll take care of the truck." Sydney didn't bother to respond, instead allowing her actions to acknowledge the order as she hopped out of the car and ran to the building. She could hear the Lexus peeling out behind her.

Sydney slowed as she reached the front door. It was glass, so she could clearly see that it was safe inside. At the same time, she knew she had to proceed with caution. She was on Felicia's turf now. Considering Sydney had already lost their first fight together on neutral ground, she was going to have to be extra careful here. Of course she planned to use the prior loss to motivate her fight now.

Sydney opened the door and stepped inside. It was a typical office setting, being used for atypical purposes. Considering the space was likely only set up for the production of Sway, Sydney doubted that Lowell's offices took up too much of the building. He wasn't the type to have housed more than one illegal operation in any one place. So at least she wouldn't have to search the entire five-story building. Felicia would stay in the area with which she was familiar.

There wasn't a doubt in Sydney's mind that Felicia was still in the building. She wouldn't have tried to sneak out the back to get away. She would have suspected by now what had happened to Lowell and would want to take her revenge.

The only way Sydney could have found out about this building was to return to the compound and get the information out of Lowell. Knowing that the man would never give up the lab willingly, Felicia would naturally assume the worst. In this case, she'd be right.

Considering the lethal weapons system believed to be in place at Lowell's compound had turned out to be nothing but a ruse, Sydney doubted that security was all that intensive at the lab. Suspecting that all that was in place was a standard alarm, which would be redundant after the commotion they had caused outside, Sydney moved through the halls swiftly but cautiously.

The first four offices she passed were empty. A quick search of each confirmed that fact. That left only two doors at the end of the hall. One must have been the lab. The other would be storage. Either could have any number of traps waiting to be sprung. Sydney considered waiting for Felicia to come to her or even finding a way to make that happen. But she ultimately decided that the direct route was often the best.

Sydney kicked in the door to her left. It flew open into a darkened room lined with empty shelves. Leading with her gun, Sydney flipped on the light to see if Felicia was hiding in the shadows. She wasn't. There was absolutely nothing in the room. Her earlier assumption had been right. Felicia had moved out the entire shipment of Sway.

With all the rooms cleared but one, Sydney moved to the door on her right. Once again she kicked it in, and once again she was met with darkness. This time when she flipped the light switch, nothing happened. This was obviously the place.

The light spilling in from the hall revealed a typical lab with long black tables lined with glass beakers, test tubes, and the like. From what Sydney could tell from the doorway, it looked like all of the drug-making ingredients had been cleared out and only the equipment was left behind. Otherwise the place had been emptied of any real evidence that an illegal operation had been taking place there. It could have easily been some kind of legal laboratory making prescription drugs that were just as illegal to send across the border into the States.

Sydney had to give some credit to the now-deceased drug lord. Considering how quickly the place had been emptied and made to look legitimate, Lowell sure knew how to anticipate any problems and prepare accordingly. Too bad he couldn't foresee his own death.

Knowing that Felicia had the upper hand in the dark room, Sydney tried to even the odds a bit by putting the woman off her game from the start. "I don't want to have to fight you again, Felicia," Sydney called into the room. "Why don't you just give yourself up? David is dead. His empire is about to be taken down by the DEA. You offer to help them dismantle it and you might cut down on your sentence."

There was no response, not that Sydney had expected one. Thankfully there wasn't any gunfire, either. The only thing left to do was enter the dark room and hope that Felicia didn't have any Sway on her, in whatever form it came in.

Leading with her gun, Sydney carefully stepped into the room. She couldn't hear anything but her own breathing. It was possible that Felicia had hidden somewhere else in the building and was using this room as a trap, but something told Sydney that the woman was in there—Felicia would want to take on the person she probably now blamed for Lowell's death—and she was right. After Sydney had taken only a few steps inside, Felicia sprung out from behind a table and kicked the gun out of Sydney's hand.

Sydney spun in the direction of the kick, with her fists raised and already blocking Felicia's punches. Sydney guessed the woman must have run out of bullets when she was firing on Lowell's Lexus. Poor planning on Felicia's part had worked to Sydney's advantage. She just hoped that she could make the most of that upper hand. She was looking forward to a fair fight with the absence of household appliances.

Felicia picked up a large glass beaker and swung it at Sydney's head. Sydney ducked as the glass slipped out of Felicia's hand and smashed against the wall.

"What is it with you and props?" Sydney asked as she leaned on the table behind her and kicked Felicia in the stomach with both feet, sending the woman backward and into the table across the way.

Sydney could see the pain of impact register on Felicia's face, but the woman recovered quickly, picking up a heavy metal chair and throwing it at Sydney. A quick dive to the left kept Sydney safe for the moment, until Felicia took a running jump at her. Sydney countered by grabbing Felicia's leg and using the woman's own momentum to throw her over the table behind Sydney.

Turning, Sydney hopped up on the table. Before she could jump down on Felicia on the other side, the woman was up and ready to continue the fight. Using the higher level as an advantage, Sydney kicked Felicia in the face. With a howl of pain, Felicia managed to grab Sydney's foot and pull. Sydney fell backward off the table but was able to turn the fall into a back flip, landing squarely on her feet.

"Impressive," Felicia said. But she wasn't done using objects in her fight. Felicia grabbed something from the storage locker behind her and slid back across the table with it, kicking Sydney in the gut and sending her stumbling backward. That's when Sydney realized what it was Felicia had in her hand: an acetylene torch.

Felicia pulled a lighter out of her jacket and held it up to the torch, igniting the gas. A flame of blue light shot out of the torch in Sydney's direction. Felicia continued toward her, holding the torch in front of her and swinging it threateningly. Sydney dropped left and right to keep away from the flame. With each move, she turned to scan the darkened room. It didn't take long for her to find what she had been looking for. The question was, how would she get there?

Dropping back, Sydney flipped herself over the nearest table and ran to the far side of the room, grabbing the metal chair that Felicia had thrown at her along the way. Whoever had designed the lab must have known exactly what Sydney was going to need, because she couldn't have asked for a better setup. The row of Bunsen burners ran along the table at the far end of the room. Each of the burners was attached to a gas line, and each of those lines met at a connector point on the wall with a protruding valve that would regulate the gas flow.

Thinking she had Sydney on the run, Felicia heedlessly followed with her torch leading the way. Sydney swung the heavy metal chair wildly as Felicia approached, but the woman was able to keep clear of the chair's path. She turned up the torch to its highest setting and waited for Sydney to make her move, but Sydney already had Felicia where she wanted her: with the gas valve on the wall between the two of them.

"Seriously, Felicia," Sydney said. "Give yourself up. This isn't going to end well for you."

"If David's dead, then it's already over," Felicia said and dove forward.

Sydney picked up the metal chair and slammed it into the gas valve, then ducked out of the way. The gas that shot out of the pipe ignited from Felicia's torch and engulfed the woman in flames. Sydney could hear the screams behind her as she rolled under the tables and fled the room.

From the hall, Sydney watched as the sprinkler system quickly kicked in, but it was too late to save Felicia.

The Lexus fishtailed as Weiss sped out of the parking lot. Skid marks pointed him in the direction he needed to go. In the brief time it took him to get out of the business park, the truck had already been swallowed up in the night. On the bright side, the route the driver had taken was the way Weiss had come. There were few turnoffs up ahead and even fewer places the truck driver could try to lose him.

Weiss pressed on the gas as he sped along the road. He did a quick check of the few side streets that split off from the main thoroughfare. Nothing was lurking down them that he could see. He quickly came up on the truck ahead of him.

True, it could have been any white panel truck, but this one was tearing down the road well in excess of the speed limit in the middle of the night. Considering it must have been full of Sway and assorted equipment, Weiss was impressed that the thing could move that fast. But it was no match for the sporty stolen car, even with a smashed rear.

Weiss accelerated as he caught up to the truck. Even on the empty road he wasn't going to start a gun battle unless he was forced into one. No, he had to find another way to take out the truck. The one thing he knew for sure was that if he was going to do that, he'd have to be the vehicle up in front, which would take some maneuvering to manage.

The road had two lanes going in either direction. There were also thin shoulders on the sides, bordered by metal guardrails that ran along the road. There was plenty of room to get past, if the truck would let him. Weiss guessed the truck driver had figured that out as well, because he had started swerving slightly across the road as if he was warning Weiss not to even try it. But Agent Eric Weiss was tired of people telling him what to do.

Weiss cut the wheel to the left, crossing into the oncoming traffic lanes. Conveniently, at the late hour, there was no oncoming traffic. He pushed the pedal almost to the floor, but the truck swerved in front of him, clipping the front of the Lexus with the truck's bumper—right at the place someone had stuck a "How's My Driving?" sticker.

Weiss eased up on the gas slightly and cut right. The truck driver countered with his own move, swinging the vehicle right as well. The move was clearly made too quickly, because the truck started to veer from the weight of the Sway. The driver managed to counter the move and held steady on the road.

Knowing the truck didn't have nearly the maneuverability of the Lexus, Weiss decided to let gravity work for him. He began haphazardly swinging the car on alternating sides of the road, forcing the truck driver to do the same, with less and less success each time. The panel truck was running the risk of tipping with each swing across the road. Weiss figured that a couple more swerves should do it.

Caught up in the moment, Weiss didn't see the lights of the oncoming car until he pulled to the left one last time. The headlights were immediately upon him. In the split second he had to react, Weiss knew that he couldn't get back to the right in time without clipping the oncoming car. Considering he was going at a speed that could do a considerable amount of damage, Weiss continued his move to the left, crossing fully in front of the oncoming car and onto the shoulder of the road. The screech of metal upon metal rang out through the night as the Lexus scraped against the guardrail.

Combined with the damage to the trunk from earlier, this was the second car he had wrecked in one night. But the wreckage wasn't over yet. As Weiss tried to put himself back on the road, the panel truck crossed over to his side and slammed him back into the guardrail. Stuck between a truck and a hard place, Weiss tried to use the Lexus to push back, but it was no use against the weight of the truck.

Sparks flew around him and the Lexus crunched under the pressure. The mirrors were ripped off both sides of the car. Wheel covers went flying. Weiss could feel the rear bumper dragging. The truck continued to smash into him, trying to force him through the rail and off the road, which would have ended in a drop into a deep ditch.

Weiss knew what he had to do. There was only one way to ensure his safety and stop the truck. He just had to time it exactly right.

The truck squeezed up against the car once again, forcing the Lexus's passenger side door to buckle inward. When the truck veered to the right again so it could come at him with another blow, Weiss released the gas pedal and tapped lightly on the brake, just enough to let the truck get ahead of him. As the truck's momentum carried it into the guardrail, Weiss floored it, swinging around to the right and in front of the truck.

Finally Weiss was where he wanted to be. Now he just had to figure out how to use his position to his advantage. The truck driver didn't seem to want to wait for Weiss to figure it out though, because the guy slammed his grill into what was left of the rear of the Lexus. Rather than trying to get away, Weiss continued to ride up against the grill of the truck. He knew it was dangerous, but it was the only way to force the truck to slow down.

Weiss was tempted to hit the brakes, but he feared the truck would flip him or roll right over him. He checked the speedometer and saw they were going in excess of ninety miles an hour. He didn't even think the truck could go that fast.

Weiss saw the road curve up ahead, followed by a short drop before an empty field. He was immediately struck with inspiration.

It's time to check out what's left of the Lexus's features, he thought.

Weiss allowed his eyes to go off the road for a brief moment as he checked out the dashboard. He quickly found the button he had been looking for. Once again, his timing would be crucial. With only a city block to go before the tight curve, he pressed the magic button. Almost immediately, the locks disengaged on the convertible top and it started to rise. As soon as it was only inches from the car's metal frame, the wind pulled it up and ripped it off what was left of the bent and broken hinge.

The top flew back, covering the window of the panel truck just in time for the driver to misjudge the turn. Weiss pulled a hard right as he swung the car away from the front of the truck. The panel truck continued on, smashing through the guardrail at full speed. The metal rail buckled and became a ramp, sending the truck up into the air before it came crashing down.

Weiss pulled the car over into a screeching stop. He pulled out his gun and went to check on the driver. There clearly must have been more than just Sway in the back of the truck though, because before Weiss could even reach it, the truck exploded in a huge fireball.

Weiss raced to the front of the vehicle to see if he could save the driver, but it was too late. The entire truck was quickly engulfed in flames. The driver was dead, and what Weiss assumed to be Lowell's entire stock of Sway had been destroyed.

Mr. Sloane is not *going to like that,* Weiss thought as he watched the truck continue to burn.

CHAPTER 21

LOS ANGELES

"We have to assume the disks with the stolen files were in the truck when it exploded," Weiss reported as he wrapped up the mission debriefing for Sloane in the man's private office. "We found nothing on the computers in Lowell's compound or in the lab."

"So, along with all the existing samples of Sway, we also lost the FBI files the drug had been based upon," Slone said. Weiss couldn't help but think that the man was rubbing it in more than clarifying the point. He wasn't really saying anything that couldn't have been inferred from Weiss's original statement.

"Yes," Weiss said succinctly. He still remembered talking back to Sloane while in the cabin. He was hoping that Sloane didn't remember or, more important, wasn't going to hold it against him.

"And Lowell and Felicia are both dead," Sloane added. "Has there been any luck finding the scientists who worked on the project for Lowell?"

"According to the files on Lowell's computer, the scientists were killed once Lowell had the formula. I guess he wanted to make sure that he was the only person in the world with the directions for making Sway. Independent intel we've secured confirmed that the people are dead."

"And with them, any chance of re-creating the drug," Sloane said. "Something I know that my daughter doesn't mind."

"Yes, she did make her feelings on that one pretty clear." Weiss laughed, before he realized what he was doing. "Um . . . sorry, sir."

"While the mission did not meet its intended goal you did succeed in keeping the FBI research from being exposed and contained the potential threat that Sway represented," Sloane noted. "And you managed to return with all the members of your team intact, while exposing a DEA mole. Ultimately, the end result can be considered a success."

"Really?" Weiss said, in shock. "That's it?"

"Is there something more you were expecting?" Sloane asked.

"No, sir," Weiss said as he quickly stood. "Not at all." He beat a hasty retreat out of the room before Sloane had a chance to bring up anything else.

Weiss could feel the smile on his own face as he walked back to his desk. He was considerably happier than he had been in days.

"I take it the mission brief went well," Vaughn said as he fell into step with his friend.

"I did a great job," Weiss said, still beaming. "Sloane told me I did a great job."

Vaughn stopped in his tracks, forcing Weiss to stop as well. "He did?" Vaughn asked. "Arvin Sloane said you did a 'great job'?"

"Well, that part was implied," Weiss explained. "But he said the mission was a success, which is pretty much the same thing."

For some reason, Vaughn was laughing. "Okay, I'll give you that. Sloane acknowledging your success is more than I ever would have expected."

"Damn right!" Weiss said. "So now I can date

his daughter without any fear of intimidation or punishment."

Vaughn rolled his eyes. "Yeah. You go on believing that. Here." He handed Weiss a computer disk. "It's the files off Lowell's computer. We've wiped anything that makes a reference to Sway in correspondence or whatever. You can give this to Agent Parker so the DEA can mop up the rest of Lowell's business."

"Thanks," Weiss said as he took the disk. He had already sat down with Parker and the DEA team to go over their brief, explaining how they—with no help from Homeland Security or any other agency—had managed to take down Lowell's organization. Parker wasn't crazy about covering up the truth, but Weiss made it clear that this was the only way to proceed.

With multiple deaths, exchanges of gunfire on public property, numerous destroyed vehicles, and an exploding warehouse, APO needed some way to explain the situation after the fact. Once they had taken Hughes into custody and ensured she wouldn't talk about what little she knew, they had effectively wiped any trace of APO's involvement in the matter and, just as important, any mention of the drug Sway. As far as the DEA was concerned, Hughes had died in the explosion. All that was missing from Parker's case was the evidence that justified his reasons for going in and taking out Lowell. That information was now securely in Weiss's hands and would be couriered to Washington that afternoon.

All in all, his mission had been a success. And now he was going to celebrate by taking Nadia out to dinner.

"Are you ready?" he asked as he found his girlfriend waiting for him at her desk.

Nadia turned to him and eagerly asked the question of the hour. "How did the briefing go?"

"Very well," Weiss said. "In fact, Mr. Sloane and I are going golfing together next week to talk about possible opportunities for advancement in the organization."

"Good to see you've still got your sense of humor," Nadia said.

"What? You don't believe me?"

Sydney watched as her sister and Weiss put on their coats and left for an evening out on the town. They had invited her and Vaughn to come out with them, but Sydney just wanted to go home and relax in the tub, blast some loud music, and maybe have a good cry.

It wasn't easy for her to deal with the things she faced every day on her job. Shifting loyalties and horrifying betrayals were the order of the day in her line of work. Even her own parents had done what had seemed to be intentionally cruel things to her throughout her life in the line of so-called duty. But less than forty-eight hours earlier she had tried to kill one of her closest friends and send her sister and the man she loved to their deaths. Even though all the actions had been done against her will, she couldn't help but hold herself accountable.

Sydney had been able to mostly ignore her feelings for the past two days. Tying up the mission and working with Agent Parker on the cover-up had taken most of her attention. It was easy to push what she had done to the back of her mind. But now that she had written her brief and her workday was done, all she could see when she closed her eyes was the image of Nadia before the screen had gone to static. She could feel Weiss pulling her off poor Agent Parker, who had taken the brunt of the attack. She could remember what it was like to have no control over her actions.

Only Dixon truly understood what she was going through. Apparently he had done things almost as unthinkable as she had, by revealing everything there was to know about the APO unit. Sydney was the only person to whom he had told the truth about what he had said to Lowell. That was not something he was about to put in his mission report. They were both grateful that Lowell had taken those secrets to his grave. If only Sydney were so lucky and no one else had known about her actions. And now she had to live with it, no matter how much she tried to put it out of her mind.

Maybe I should have taken Weiss and Nadia up on their invitation to go out tonight, she thought.

"Penny for your thoughts," Vaughn said as he sat on the edge of her desk.

"You'd think by now that would be the last offer anyone would make around this place," Sydney said, trying to make light of her emotional instability at the moment.

"Yeah," Vaughn said. "Forget I said that. Are you about wrapped up here?"

"More or less," Sydney said as she logged out of her computer and started putting things away in her messenger bag to take home with her.

"Hey," Vaughn said, taking her hand and stopping her from her busy work. "I hope you don't mind, but Weiss said something to me earlier."

Sydney worried that he wanted to talk about the Sway situation. He had been very good about leaving the subject alone earlier because she had made it clear she wasn't ready to talk about it. Maybe Weiss had explained to him what it was like to be there firsthand and Vaughn was going to force her to talk about it now.

"About my mother," Vaughn mentioned haltingly.

Sydney would have laughed if she'd had the energy. She had totally forgotten about her conversation with Weiss about never having met Vaughn's mother. Sydney wasn't sure if she was grateful or annoyed that he didn't want to bring up the other issue. The whole thing about meeting Vaughn's mom just seemed so silly now.

"I don't want you to think that I've been keeping you from her on purpose," Vaughn said.

"No. Not at all."

"It's just, things have been so crazy around here," he continued. "Things are *always* so crazy around here."

"So I've noticed."

"It just never seemed like the right time," he said.

"I know," Sydney said. "That's why I never mentioned it. I didn't want you to feel pressured."

"No. You're right," he said. "You should have met her by now. We were almost engaged once. It's crazy that you haven't met my mom yet."

"Well, how would you explain the fact that we had to break off our engagement because I went missing for two years while tracking down artifacts related to a fifteenth-century prophet?" It was only when Sydney said it out loud that she truly appreciated the humor in those two horrific years.

"Oddly enough," he said, "considering my father's history, she'd probably understand."

Sydney just nodded.

"So, here's what we're going to do," Vaughn said. "Mom's out of the country at the moment, but when she gets back and things calm down around here, I'll take you to meet her."

"Really?" Sydney asked. "When things calm down around here? So you're never going to take me to meet her?"

Vaughn laughed. "Soon," he said. "I promise."

"I'm going to hold you to that," she said as she

got up and kissed him, not caring if anyone in the glass-walled offices was looking.

"Now, why don't we go catch up with Weiss and Nadia," he said. "They mentioned something about a fun night of sushi and bowling."

"I don't think so," Sydney replied. "I'm not really in the mood for anything but a quiet night soaking in the bathtub."

"Well now, that's okay too," Vaughn said, clearly taking it as an invitation.

ABOUT THE AUTHOR

Paul Ruditis is the author of the Alias novel *Vigilance* and the official episode guide for the first four seasons of the series: Alias: *Authorized Personnel Only*. He has also written and contributed to numerous books based on such notable TV shows as Buffy: *The Vampire Slayer*, *Angel*, *Charmed*, *Star Trek*, and *The West Wing*. He lives in Burbank, California